Also by Adrienne Nash

'A Strange Life', my autobiography.

'Trudi', 'Trudi in Paris', 'Trudi and Simon', 'Trudi without Simon'.

'Tina G',

'The Cellar',

'A Time to be Brave'.

Breakdown.

By

Adrienne Nash

About Me.

Hi. I spent half my life as a boy as described in my autobiography, 'A Strange Life'. A short while ago someone who read it said 'What was so strange about that?' Well he is a 'straight' man, very content in his skin and seems to have no conception of the torment suffered by transsexuals, denied the right to react and act in what seems an alien world.

Unfortunately I was born in a time when changing sex was unknown. Yes people cross dressed, even lived their lives as the opposite to their natal sex, but it was done surreptitiously and men were liable to arrest, conviction and imprisonment for 'impersonating women.' Not so for women dressing as men.

The Health Service sought to cure me, with offers to put me to sleep for months to see if I would wake up 'right', their exact words, or give me 'aversion therapy' which included electric shocks and ridiculously, suggested amateur dramatics as though dressing up was all I sought.

None of their treatments were effective, so in the early 1970's the World's medical profession decided the only answer is to change the body to match the mind and character.

Some churches do not recognise sex change, yet they have no alternative therapy to offer, but then religious leaders are notorious for arriving at wrong conclusions.

This novel is fiction and the characters do not represent any known real persons, unfortunately!

Please review it if you like it.

Breakdown

Chapter 1.

I don't know where to begin really. Oh yes they always say, the place to start is at the beginning, but for me, was it my birth, my schooling or the death of my parents? Was it finding out that dad had been a fraudster, playing the millionaire with other peoples' money? I don't know. There are so many things I don't know, why for example, could I not cope after my parents' tragic and early death, their car found at the bottom of a ravine on a little used Alpine pass? Why were they on that route? Was it suicide and was it a pact or did mum have no choice? Had my father as usual, made the decision and thereby murdered my mum?

The newspapers and TV had found a new story to push, day after day, my father's past, the discovery that he was bankrupt in all but name. The vision in my mind of the car going over the precipice and my mother's horrified, screaming face haunted me in my dreams and yes, in my days too. This image I fear, will shadow me all my life.

I have mixed thoughts. Father just loved driving and he liked wild places. He had no fear of heights and he rather liked a dare. Mother hated heights, she wasn't that keen on wild places either. Mum was a town girl, cathedrals; old houses; museums and art galleries; malls; these were her idea of a successful touring holiday.

How and why had the car gone over the edge? Dad was a good driver, skilled. He had in his younger days been a rally driver for one of the lesser teams. He had driven in the Welsh Rally and the Monte Carlo, Swedish and even the East African until he met mum and she became pregnant. There could really only be one answer to why the car had left the road.

He loved cars but he was not a good businessman. He had put his money into a car dealership. When he died, the business folded. The accountants found the books were fictitious and he actually owed over a million personally and much more in the business. There had been no figure set on that yet; accountants are still trying to calculate the total. The manufacturer he had represented took everything, all the business premises, the family home, and the house I occupied while at Uni. I am left a penniless orphan.

When it happened I'd been at university just over a year, living in the house provided by father, with three other guys. It was dad's name on the deeds, so it too was taken. My housemates found other houses. I had a breakdown. I spent three months under medication with an aunt, my mum's older sister.

She was kind but eccentric but found me, in my depressed state, difficult. I was, I mean I could not help it, but a nineteen year old man crying, is not a pretty sight and after a time, who would want to throw their arms around me because that human touch actually did not comfort me, so what would be the point. When I overheard aunt Ellen and uncle Richard discussing me and sighing, I knew I had to go.

An old school friend who went up to university with me, had phoned regularly to see how I was. She, Gemma was in a rented house with two other girls. We had been good pals at school, no romance, just like minds who helped each other out in our studies. She was a cut above, and even though I was what was referred to as an oddball, queer, sissy, Gem stood by me. I did not identify with the boys. We were both known as swats, teachers' pets at school. We were not popular in a school not known for its academic successes.

Since the breakdown, Gemma had phoned at least once a week. Last week she told me they had a small fourth bedroom and I was welcome to it until I could find somewhere else.

In desperation I rang her and she made the offer once more. 'Thanks Gemma. Really, I mean I'm not good company. Do you want to run that by your house mates first?'

'So you are interested. Well that is a good sign. I have mentioned you Alex, and we sort of discussed it, but yeah, I'll talk to them tonight, and get a definite yea or nay, phone you tomorrow. You are not going to do anything stupid are you? You're not; I hate even saying the word, suicidal? I don't think we could cope with that.'

'No, I realise that this is a stage in my life and I have to get over it. I want to get my degree, because now I know I haven't dad's money to fall back on, I have to be a success. In any case, I want to be a designer and that means finishing my course. As it is, I think I may have to do another year to catch up. It will be good to be with people my own age.'

'Well at least you are feeling more positive. It is no good dwelling on tragedy, it only damages you. We are all sympathetic Alex but we will try to get you out of your pit of despond, not pamper and pander.'

'I think that is what I need, some normality.'

'Good! And you will have to pay rent, I mean not straight away, but you can't live here for free Alexander, it wouldn't be fair to my mates. We all pay into a budget too, for food etcetera.'

'Of course, I'll have to get a job.'

'That might be difficult. I'll keep my ears and eyes open for an opportunity. One more thing and something we have never really discussed, we always danced around the subject. If you are gay, then we would not want a series of gay lovers coming and going. Are you?'

'No I'm not, not as far as I know. I like girls, I like their company. I don't think I even understand boys.'

'OK. I'll phone you as soon as I have had a chat with Sue and Jacquie.'

Chapter 2.

Gemma didn't phone next day and I fretted. I'd taken a long walk in the afternoon through the woods and down to the river Mole. From there I made my way up a beech tree covered slope where no one seemed to go.

I lowered my backpack to the leaf-strewn floor in a hollow. I took off my sweater and tea shirt, then trousers and socks, until I was just in my underwear, suspender belt, stockings, pants, bra and a slip. I danced like a ballerina, bare feet in the mostly dry rustling leaves, wind blowing in my long hair. Blonde tresses floated across my face as I pirouetted. For a time I just lay in a dry leafy hollow, listening to the wind in the trees and the sounds of the forest, the coo of wood pigeons and a blackbird singing brightly. I lay on my back in my sweet sheltered hollow, looking up through the bare winter branches and watched clouds scudding across the sky. I was hyper alert to any foreign sounds that might spell discovery or danger. Would I ever be happy I wondered? I never had been, not really, there just seemed to be something lacking in me, apart from this, my obsession.

I did not respect myself. I knew that cross-dressing went on, but it was not a label I wished applied to me. There were other labels too, pervert, failure, sissy, words that my father had used in his tirades when I failed to please.

I found relationships difficult, I had been as a child, really shy, and I mean blushing shy, not good in a boy. I was also an only child, only and lonely, living in a converted barn about a mile from the village. I had always wanted to be a girl, not something my father would have understood. I think mum knew but tried to ignore it, to keep, as she saw it, the peace within our small family.

Frightened of discovery, I dressed, wearing my boy things over the top. I walked mobile in my hand, waiting for a call from Gemma and it did not come. When I returned I asked aunt whether there had been a phone call, but no luck there either. I was disappointed and I thought the worst. Gemma's pals had said no, I surmised, and she didn't want to tell me the bad news.

I went to bed early. I took a needle, and flamed it with my gas lighter. I pushed it through my penile skin and cried. I took one of the sleeping pills I had been prescribed.

I awoke to wind lashing the windowpane, actually drumming on it, driving in upon that side of the house, the strands of Virginia creeper smacking the pane. I got up and showered in the family bathroom that was used solely by me as Aunt and Uncle had their en suite. I decided to shave, something I did only rarely because my facial hair grew slowly still and was quite fine and sparse.

I dressed and went down for breakfast. Aunt made me porridge and while I ate that, she boiled two eggs served with soldiers.

'How are things today Alex. You seem more down after your walk yesterday.'

'I'm waiting for a call from my friend Gemma, but she hasn't phoned. I'm a bit disappointed.' Of course it wasn't only that, I was disappointed with myself that I had indulged in my obsession and then punished myself. I knew, because I was quite sane although troubled, that unless the pressure was removed, I would self-destruct. I hoped that living with a household of girls would help. Certainly the constrictions of my own house with three male lodgers had not been helpful, in fact it had been hateful. Living with Aunt and Uncle was equally difficult.

'Perhaps she has been busy or hasn't had an opportunity. Is it important to you?'

'Oh it's just the chance of a room. If I get a room I can get back to my studies and I think if I do that, I will be able to shake off my depression. I hate being like this Aunt Ellen. I'm sorry I have been a burden, a wet blanket on the house.'

'Well it has not been easy, but it has been understandable. Bad enough for me losing my sister, but for you to lose both parents, home and roof over your head. It's been an awful time for you. Is there news of your dog and cat?'

'Mum's cleaner kept feeding them for a week and then they were sent to an animal shelter. They have been rehomed.'

'Oh dear, you were so fond. So you feel well enough to get back to college?'

'Yes, I think I need hard work, bury myself in it with some young people around me. I can't thank you enough for having me, both of you.'

'The least we could do and don't think you have to rush away but I think you are right, you need work and company of young friends. You know Alexander, hard work is the best medicine for depression. This Gemma, is she a close friend?'

'Not like I think you mean. We were at school together and stuck together in the face of the philistines, the idiots who thought school was for mucking about.'

'Well I have a job for you today Alex, something to occupy you. I want you to mow both lawns, they have grown in this mild weather. You know how to use the mower?'

'Oh I can do that OK.'

That occupied most of the morning. Their back lawn was huge, about three tennis courts with ornamental trees set in neat circles. The mower was an old twenty-four inch Webb, but it cut well. The main problem was emptying the box. Two runs up and down and it was full, I then needed to empty it on the heap another fifty metres at the bottom of the garden. I also had to do all the edging and leave it tidy.

I kept my phone in my pocket, but there was no call. I debated calling Gemma, but resisted the urge. I knew if she had news she would phone.

In the afternoon I clipped part of the large yew hedge that bordered the neighbours. More clearing up. By five I was quite exhausted but it had been good to be occupied. I walked across the mown lawn and felt pride in the accomplishment.

Just as we sat down to dinner my phone started buzzing and jumping. I excused myself and went into the hall.

15

'Alex? Gemma. OK Alex, you can have the room. It is only small, you have a bed in there and a desk to work at and there is a sort of built in tallboy, but that is about all. We all use it but we can get our stuff out. There are rules. The rent, we thought £40 a week? Then this is a girl's house, so respect our privacy and if we occasionally appear half dressed, try not to leer. You have to be tidy. You have to be clean and you share the chores. I don't think you are a smelly boy but you have to get with the programme and be as clean as us.'

'No problem Gemma. You know that.'

'Yes I do, but I just had to make the point. The girls are here now with me, listening on speaker, and they want to be sure you know the ground rules. So you promise?'

'I'll obey the rules. I just can't thank you enough, all of you. When can I come?'

'It's Wednesday. Say Friday, gives us time to clear the room and that gives us all four the weekend to get used to each other.'

'Friday then, Gemma thanks and Sue and Jacquie too, thank you. Oh what time?'

'Sue and I work Friday afternoon at Pizza Hut, but Miss Moneybags will be here. Jacquie will let you in.' A shout of 'Hi I'll be here,' came over the phone distantly. It was a musical voice.

I told Aunt Ellen and Uncle Richard the news.

'Well if you are ready dear, I'm sure it's the right thing to do but keep in touch, we want to know you are well and coping.'

Friday, I packed my old BMW Mini, my last possession from mum and dad's time and set off for University.

Jacquie met me as arranged. I knew her and Sue but only slightly through my contacts with Gemma. She was an attractive girl, slightly Italian looking, dark hair, flowing, looking like polished mahogany, with some lighter strands of chestnut in it. Her eyes were blue though, quite piercing. I had an instant liking for her. She was intriguing. My immediate impression was of a bird, her fine features and quick movements gave that impression, though she was not beaky. It was hard to explain the bird thing.

'Hi I'm Jacquie Coles, you remember we met? OK Alex, I'll give a hand with your stuff.'

'I can manage thanks, about three trips should do it.'

She looked at me quizzically. 'No I'm offering. This house is a team. Just because you are a boy, don't think you are on your own. One family. You are now an honorary girl. I'll take the suitcase and leave it outside your room so you know which it is, you can bring another armful.'

She departed, lugging the suitcase across the pavement and through the front door. I grabbed a pile of bedding and followed her. When I reached the stairs she was just coming down.

'Here, I'll take those you go back to the car and prepare the next load.'

Soon everything was in and my little car was locked up safely.

'The bed is OK but you may want to get another from the second hand place down the street sometime. Here, I'll help make it up.'

She stood close to me, something she did, I mean I was used to keeping people at arms reach, she was in my space and I caught her perfume in my nostrils. I breathed it in. I would have to get some.

We made the bed and I put my few clothes in the wardrobe, a sort of tallboy with drawers and a section to hang as well. I surreptitiously put my few girlie things in a drawer and covered them with PJs.

Jacquie sat on my newly made bed and watched, chatting about her drama course. She was full of it for she had just done a spot in an advert for national TV.

'Wow Jacquie, that's good. Will that get you noticed?'

'My agent says so.'

'You have an agent already?'

'You don't get anywhere without one. You are doing fashion, surely that is much the same?'

'A bit different. I have to catch the eye of someone at the degree show. I am selling my creations more than myself.'

'Oh, I 'spose. Tea? We have some hot cross buns, would you like one? Something to keep us going until we have dinner. We thought we would all have dinner together tonight to celebrate your arrival.'

'Tea and a bun would be good, thank you. You are very kind.' Even with this exchange I felt my cheeks redden.

'You are not going to cry are you? If you do, I'll give you a good slap. Hey that's better a small smile. Come on, toasted bun, inside and out? How do you like it?'

'That's fine toasted in and out. Thank you, you are so welcoming.'

'And why wouldn't I be. As far as I am concerned you are not on trial here, you are a housemate and to a certain extent, we look after each other. When one is down we try to bring them back up.

'So this is the sitting room. The couch is quite comfy. Sue likes that chair opposite the telly, complains she gets a crick if she sits elsewhere. I don't believe her but it doesn't matter to me. Gemma usually has the other easy chair as she doesn't like TV that much, she prefers to read. So it is you and I on the sofa. It's cold now after having the door open. I'll put the gas fire on for a little while. We'll be nice and cosy.'

She made tea in an old ultramarine blue pot and rattled mugs covered in cats onto a tray. I washed my hands and looked after toasting the teacakes. I caught her smiling as if there was a private joke.

'Sorry, did I do something wrong?'

'No, you did something right. Are you sure you are a boy?'

'Last time I looked. Why?'

'You washed your hands. And your hair, it's way down your back. Are most on your course a little weird?'

'I'm weird? Oh! Fashion design? I suppose we are different, encouraged to be different and creative, depart from the norm. We have to think out of the box, blue sky all those clichés. While I guess you have to be mostly conforming, acting the normal. Some of us have tattoos and piercings, I have long hair. I don't like marking my body. Now I suppose you are going to say, ah, that explains it and you suspect I am gay.'

'Oh, are you?'

'No, but people assume anyone in fashion is.'

'So have you a girlfriend now?'

'No.' I blushed. Damn. She was so direct.

'Have you ever had one?'

'No not really.'

'Why?'

'Never met anyone special.'

'How about me? Do you fancy me?'

'Are you always like this? Are you looking for a compliment or what?'

She laughed and tossed her hair over her shoulder, looking at me from the side of her eyes. She was so vivacious, lively, the face of a beautiful animal or bird, large blue eyes, long thick dark lashes and she knew how to use these assets. Some girls I had observed, use their eyes like men, turning their head to see you, some, sexier girls, swivel their eyes, looking from below lashes or from the side of their eyes. I didn't know whether this was just her nature or whether she was being provocative, making a pass.

We took our tea into the sitting room and sat on the floor, warming ourselves before the fire.

'So do you design dresses or what?'

'We can more or less do what we want, men's casuals or suits or women's wear, from bras outwards.'

She smiled. Lovely smile, her eyes lit up. 'That must be really nice to do, really creative. I could model for you.'

22

'Well, so you could. So are you, creative I mean, what course are you on exactly, or is their just one course that covers all performing arts?'

'Drama and dance. We do a bit of singing, so we can have a go at musicals too. No it is not the same sort of creativity as dress design. I copy, what a script says or the mannerisms of someone I have seen at sometime. I am constantly noting how people behave how they sit, stand walk, smile, talk. It is all stored in here,' she pointed to her head, 'so if I need it for a character, I can draw on it, but it is basically copying. I analyse people. We are taught a bit of self-defence in case we have a fight scene, sort of how to fall, how to take a slap or punch and how to give one without hurting. That sort of thing. It's just endless fun.'

'And you are analysing me. Do you then make a judgement?'

'Don't think I am judgemental. Yes I have analysed you, don't we all when we meet someone? Instant attraction or instant dislike. I shall not say what I think yet. You look very drawn, as though you have been through the mill, and of course you have. You are quite beautiful for a boy. No don't blush; there are beautiful men, Johnny Depp, Russell Brand whether you like them and what they do. You need to smile more. Actually you are pretty rather than beautiful, and you have nicer hair. Would you let me play with it, just brush it about. It's really thick isn't it? It could be really nice if you took care of it.'

I blushed again. 'Do what you like.'

She fetched a brush and comb. 'You know you have split ends? Can I just trim it up? I promise I won't make a mess of it. You washed it this morning didn't you. I can smell the shampoo. You should find a better conditioner. It's a bit fly away. Come into the kitchen and I'll just trim the ends. I shall have to teach you about grooming.'

She produced scissors and carefully snipped away. It was all very personal and intimate. I found it quite exciting, alluring. I supposed I was just so vulnerable, starved of human touch, starved of love.

'OK. Done.' She swept the cut hair into a pan and sent it into the waste. She combed and brushed, from somewhere she produced a hair clip and put it in my hair. 'Stay there.' She disappeared and returned with a mirror. 'What do you see?' she asked smiling.

I examined my reflection and felt myself blushing again.

'I don't know what you mean, it's just me.'

'Yes you do know. Don't you think you look quite girly?'

'Well with the way you have done my hair, yes, but that's not how I usually do it.' I said a bit tersely.

'I've upset you. Here.' She removed the hairgrip. 'Sorry. Did I touch a nerve?'

'A bit, you know doing fashion design, people think..... well you can guess.'

'But a lot of the time they are right aren't they?' It's like male dancers; everyone thinks they are all gay but only about seventy per cent are. I couldn't care less. Do you like being called Alex or Alexander?'

'Either.'

'When you are famous and have your own fashion house, it will have to be Alexander, Alexander of Paris.'

'Do you always make fun of people?'

'No. I'm trying to get to know you. How about if I call you Alexandra? Shall I? Would you mind?

'Why would you?'

'Because. You are very passive, and quite reticent. I'm going to ask questions and you answer and I will also answer, like favourite colour?'

'Blue.'

'Me too. Second favourite?'

'Cerise.'

'Do you mean pink?'

'I do like pink. What are you going to read into that?'

'I said I'm not judgemental, only interested. I like pink too. See we have similar tastes. Hair colour?'

'Blonde.'

'On you or on others?'

'Well on me and I guess on girls too. But you are lovely, I mean your hair is so shiny, and pretty.'

'Yes but mine is out of a bottle, well partly. I think yours is too, though you must have done your roots recently.'

'Yesterday.'

'There. Music who do you like?' She smiled again.

'Lot's. Favourites of the moment a song called Up and Cheerleader. But I like classical too, from Beethoven to the Beatles.'

'Eclectic. Me too, but not country, too mournful, too sad. I see those endless prairies, girls in faded denim dresses, nails dirty and broken, starved of real love.'

She was so fascinating.

'Favourite painter?'

'Oh that's difficult. Lots, van Gogh in his pointillist period, Monet, Lautrec, Hockney sometimes, well lots sometimes. Not all pictures artists paint, are good paintings. I mean some Gainsboroughs are awful, and Constables too, those Stubbs horses don't look right and even the sainted Turner produced some awful stuff. I went to The Orangerie in Paris, some Renoirs there, terrible daubs. I have been to Musée d'Orsay twice, no rubbish on display there. Stunning.'

'I went there last year. We must go to some galleries together. I like art too. I think we will have a lot in common.

'I'm sorry if I have embarrassed you. I'm sure we are going to be good friends. Can I do something else with your hair?'

I didn't know what to make of her or what would come next. 'Do what you like,' I said submissively.

'Come and sit in front of me, back between my knees. But first, do you want more tea Alexandra?'

I ignored using the feminine of my name, but it sent a thrill through me. 'Yes please.'

She went to the kitchen and soon returned with a fresh mug. She set it by my side. She sat behind me and combed my hair through. 'Do you use straighteners?'

'Sometimes.'

'You know what I am doing?'

'I'm guessing you are plaiting.'

'Is that OK?'

'I don't mind. Actually I like my hair being done.'

'Hey that's a breakthrough. You have actually volunteered something personal about you. Good, we are making progress.'

I did like it; in fact sitting there with Jacquie playing with my hair was heaven. It was sensuous, the most intimate thing that had happened to me for a long, long time. I was quite turned on. She stopped.

'Put your left hand up here,' she said. She took my hand and placed the end of a pigtail into it. 'Hold that. I'll be back in a moment.'

She eased from behind me and took off up the stairs, a flash of long legs in a mini skirt. She returned and bounced into her seat behind me. She took the pigtail and I heard her fastening it with an elastic band. Then she was tying it with what I took was a ribbon. She bounced away again and returned with the mirror.

'You like?'

I looked. My reflection was even more girlish than before. 'What are you trying to do to me?'

'Just playing. Do you mind?'

'Not if you want to do it.'

'You said you liked having your hair played with.'

'I do. Actually it is really nice. I do look a bit of a girl though.'

'If I plucked your eyebrows, even more so. You have small ears and good skin. The others won't be home for two hours yet and we are having spag bol, which you and I will do. I have an idea. Can I change you into a girl, play a joke on them?'

'What do you mean?'

'Well I have done your hair. How about I do your face, just for fun.'

'OK.' I shrugged, trying to give the impression that it didn't affect me. Actually it did. It was really exciting. To use a biblical expression, my loins stirred. Why? I hoped it didn't show.

Away she scampered again returning with a make up case. She swabbed my face with a cotton pad and some liquid, then moisturised. 'You haven't much stubble, hardly anything.'

I blushed again.

'Boy or not, your eyebrows do need some treatment. I am going to pluck the stray hairs.'

She worked away, her face serious, concentrating. 'That's better.'

She applied foundation, pencilled my eyebrows, then did my eyes, lined and shadowed, mascara followed by blusher. Lastly she applied lip liner and lipstick. She leaned back critically. 'Mmm.' She said. 'OK, now to get you dressed. Stay exactly where you are and don't touch the mirror.' She turned it face down. 'I'll be back in a minute. No, I don't trust you.' She picked the mirror up and took it with her. She was back in a minute with a bundle of clothes.

'I think this has gone far enough Jacquie.'

'Oh don't back out now and spoil everything. It will be such a joke. I have got this far, don't make me take it all off again! They expect miserable Alex and they'll find instead, lovely Alexandra.'

'But I can see a bra and skirt there, even heels. I don't think I want to go that far.'

'What are you scared of? Casting off your frail masculinity?'

'It's just not normal for a man to do this.'

'I know couples who cross dress, just for fun or for a party or a trick. It's only clothes for God's sake. As an actor we do it all the time. I could play a prostitute or a murderess. Lady Macbeth or Anne of Green Gables. Or if a small company was short of an actor, a boy. Come on, be a sport.'

'OK if it means that much.'

'Good boy!' At least she was calling me a boy. Yet there was part of me really wanted to change into these clothes. Why? But I knew why. My senses were assaulted by the touch of another human and intimacy had long been absent. Her interest in me, her touch, her absence of any barriers, broke through the shell that I hid behind. I had not been this happy in a long time.

'I can't change in front of you though.'

'Why not, I know what boys look like, I have two brothers.'

'And did you dress them up too?'

'Yes actually. They thought it great fun. Well take your top off and I will help you with the bra. You can put tights on I take it and knickers?'

'Knickers? I can wear my pants.'

'No full kit or you will not get into the part. They are not terribly girlie pants, Look.' She held up some white pants, thin pink lace edging and a pink bow. My face was burning under the makeup.

She was already carefully pulling off my shirt and jumper so as not to ruin my makeup. She put the bra straps over my hands and pulled it up my arms and fastened it.

'I'll let you do the rest. No chickening. I'll start the Bolognaise.'

I looked at what she had left me. Black thick tights, a mini skirt in red, a blouse with a Peter Pan collar and a black jumper. I drew the curtains, suddenly realising that I was standing wearing a bra in full view from the street and it was now nearly dark outside. I found that quite humorous, dangerous and exciting.

I put on the knickers and felt my penis expand. Oh damn, thing has a mind of it's own I thought. I tried tucking everything down forcing it, trying to make everything disappear. My testicles vanished upwards, burying themselves inside somewhere. They did that. I knew they would come back. With blood supply cut off, my penis subsided. I pulled the knickers up tight and hoped. I struggled with the tights, pulling them up each leg bit by bit. They helped contain my male anatomy. I put the mini on and the blouse with its fiddly little pearlised buttons. And then the sweater, careful not to smudge my face. My hands were shaking.

I swore to myself. I loved it, I was in ecstasy.

Lastly I worked my feet into the shoes. They were rather tight. Shyly I went to the kitchen door and opened it. Jacquie turned.

'Oh my. If I didn't know. Moses, you are beautiful.' She turned off the gas under the pan.

'Come,' she grasped my hand, 'upstairs and see for yourself.' She more or less towed me up the staircase and into a bedroom where there was a full-length mirror.

I took in the apparition that stood there. I saw a reasonable looking girl, blushing, head downcast a little like Diana Princess of Wales had once stood in her early day photos, that dreadful engagement photo shoot when Charlie had said, 'whatever love means' I had seen on a documentary on the sad Princess last year.

'Head up chin up and stand up straight with shoulders back.'

I did as I was told. 'Bloody hell!' I said.

'Have you never cross dressed before?'

'Not since I was a child. I think I did then, but dad wanted me to get involved in cars and things.'

'What not since then? Are you sure?' She looked at me sideways. 'Hmm, I won't press you, but I do not believe you.'

I suddenly felt very vulnerable. This vivacious, rapacious girl was so perceptive and so unstoppable.

'Well come on Alexandra, we have a dinner to do. We can't stand here all night admiring your reflection.'

'I think I want to take it off.'

'Uh uh, and spoil the fun? Come on Alexandra and help get the dinner. It is a term of your lease on that room that you assist with household chores.'

She grasped my hand and made for the stairs towing me behind her.

I wanted to stay like this forever. Down in the kitchen she set me to preparing some veg. We heard the front door open and a shout of hello.

Chapter 3.

'Hi' Jacquie shouted, 'I'm in here with a friend.'

Gemma put her head in the door. 'Oh, no Alex? Where is he?'

'Don't know. This is Zandra, she's an actress.' I noticed this time she used the feminine of actor, a deliberate part of her subterfuge.

'Oh hi Zandra. She's got you working. Jacquie! I thought you were going to take care of Alex?'

'Oh I have. He's fine. Helping me cook.'

'Oh my goodness. Alex! Is this you or has Jacquie been amusing herself?

'She has been amusing herself.'

'Come here darling. Are you OK? Really Jacquie, I asked you to look after him. You changed him into a bloody girl.' There was a giggle from behind Gemma.

'Hi Zandra. Let me see.' Sue pushed her head into the kitchen. I turned to face them; putting down the pan I had filled with spinach. I put my arms out as if in resignation, my face burning beneath the makeup and did my best to smile.

'Wow, good job. I would never have known. I love the hair. She needs a bracelet and earrings. I'll get some, I have some clip ons.'

'OK girls, you have had your fun. I think I'll change.' I had to make some sort of stand I felt, for prides sake. However, if I was more certain of my sexuality it would not have mattered would it? It would just have been a great joke. Inside, I just loved it but I did not want them to know. It took me back to my childhood when such things were permitted behaviour and mother offered tender love. Later it had all become taboo, a shameful thing.

'You don't need to. Just be one of us, for tonight Alex.' Gemma said, surprising me and even Jacquie it seemed for she turned to me and raised her brows. 'There,' she said, 'approval.'

Sue arrived back and shouldered her way into the kitchen. She clipped on the earrings and fastened a bracelet round my submissive wrist. It was arousing. I hoped panties and tights would restrain my auto reactions.

Sue kissed my cheek, well each cheek. I burned up again.

'OK girls, out of our kitchen while Zandra and I finish off. Dinner in five. Oh red or white wine?' She asked me.

'Either.'

'Then I think we will make a night of it. Get the white from the fridge and we will have this red too. Frozen tiramisu for afters, I'll leave that out to defrost.' Strain the veg Zandra, and we are ready to go.'

The girls had laid the table and we carried in the main course.

'Well you two,' Gemma said, 'you girls have been busy.'

I blushed again. 'I'm not usually like this.' I insisted, 'I'm Alex.'

'But tonight you are the delectable Zandra,' Sue said, with an amused smile, helping us all to spaghetti. 'Honest I would not have known. Wasted.'

'What?' I asked stupidly, now liking the attention of these lively girls.

'Your looks. I have forgotten what you look like as a boy.' Gemma said.

'Not you too. I thought at least you would protect me.'

'Oh no, you look after yourself *Zandra*. Smile, you know you have enjoyed the attention and we have taken your mind off everything haven't we?' She took a photo. I blinked after the flash.

I did not answer immediately. 'Actually the best afternoon and evening, not just since the tragedy but for a long time.'

Gemma smiled and touched my nylon clad knee. 'Glad we have helped.'

The evening went from the dining table to being sprawled out, watching videos, girlie films which I liked. In the space of a few hours I had become part of this family, an honorary girl, a plaything.

At bedtime, Sue took my make up off with remover and surprisingly moisturised my face, then left me to brush my teeth. I said goodnight and went to my room. I looked in the mirror. I still looked girlie. I still had the plait. I turned my head and it flipped like a whip. I felt the weight of it. I took off the clothes, reluctantly, and folded them carefully. I went to bed in the pants. It had been the best day for months, even years. Tomorrow I would be Alexander again. It had been fun but I knew who I was. Alexander, no longer tragic, but still confused.

Chapter 4.

Saturday and the girls were up late. I made breakfast from what I found, laid the table for four and cleared up the kitchen from last night. When it was all spic and span, I got the vacuum out and did the downstairs. I even dusted. I remembered the terms of my lease as Jacquie had put it. I had to pull my weight.

Jacqueline was first to appear, in pyjamas, her hair mussed.

'Hi Alex, was that the vacuum I heard? I thought I was having a nightmare.' She looked around the kitchen. 'You have been busy. So what is for breakfast, have you made that too?'

'No, but we have eggs, I can do fried, scrambled or boiled. Fried can be sunny or over easy or fried to a frazzle. Oh I forgot, poached on toast too. Or porridge or just coffee or tea.'

'You really are a girl Alex.' I must have looked embarrassed, for she added, 'I'm only teasing. You are very sweet. Sorry about yesterday, I was awful to you. I don't know what comes over me sometimes.'

'It's OK. Actually I enjoyed all the attention, something I have not had for quite a long time. I needed a bit of bullying, leg pulling and pampering. You did all that. I forgot to feel sorry for myself.'

'And today?'

'I feel much more positive.'

'I'm going to have poached on toast, then I am going to browse the Mall. Why don't you come with me?'

"I'll do the egg and make the toast. The Mall! I could browse for any jobs at the same time, see if there are any zero hours going.'

'Good plan. So are you going like that or what?'

'What do you mean?'

'I mean the pigtail.'

'Oh I had forgot.'

'Yeah right.'

'I'll undo it.'

'You don't have to. After all you are a fashionista, a fashion student. You are encouraged to be different aren't you? I dare you to keep the pigtail.'

I thought a moment. Compared to most 'fashionistas' as apparently we were nicknamed, I was pretty square, uncool, my body unmarked by tattoos or piercings. I did not admit to myself, all the times I had self-harmed. Fashion students had all sorts of weird hairstyles from Mohican to shaved up one side, even a few pigtails. I had wondered whether tattoos and very weird hair were a sort of self harm.

'Yeah OK. Easy dare.'

'You are quite different today, as though you have found yourself.'

'I think I have. I think I'm in love with being with you girls. Yesterday was brill.'

She looked at me again, sideways, as I placed her egg and toast in front of her. 'Thanks Zand.'

'You are a great tease Miss Jacquie,'

'And you are a pretty girl, Miss Zandra Gregson.'

I laughed; it was impossible to be angry with this vivacious girl. She ate as I drank my tea sitting opposite. Somehow today I felt less inhibited.

'Mmm. That was good thanks Zand. Do you mind if I call you Zandra?'

'Why would you want to? Except to tease?'

'Because...I hope you won't mind my saying, but you still look so girlie. I'm sorry, I don't mean to hurt you, but I say what I think most of the time. Actually you fascinate me. Anyway, I know we are going to be great friends. I'll get ready. Leave in fifteen? You know you can be whoever you want to be here. You are very girly, I mean the way you managed that mini skirt. Boys would just open their knees and let everyone see what they had up there. Not you. Do you want to do your face first?' She was teasing again.

I chose to ignore rather than refute her observations. 'Fifteen minutes, will be fine.'

'Need me to do your makeup?'

'There you go again.' How I wanted to say, 'yes please Jacqueline.' Instead I laughed and blushed. I loved this teasing over my sexuality. 'Go and get yourself ready.'

I cleared up and washed the things we had used so that when the others came down, it was all tidy for them. I went to my room and looked at myself in the mirror. Well the pigtail was a bit of a statement. A ponytail was one thing, so awful on older men but frequently seen on arty men. A plaited pigtail was something else. I studied my face. While my eyebrows looked more defined than they had been, they were I thought, just passable for a fellow my age. If the rest of my face was female, then I could not see it. I just saw a rather frail young man, not even handsome. I looked as though I had really been through a bad illness, slight rings below my eyes, skin transparent and pale. I shrugged, selected some light pumps and put my last twenty in my pocket. That was the total asset I had left.

We met on the landing.

'How about some eyeliner?' she said, 'That's something boys do.'

I considered. 'OK.'

'Come.' We entered her bedroom. She had a large double bed, it was quite girly and it smelled of her, her perfume and whatever else she used. She sat me on her stool and deftly applied eyeliner.

I turned to the mirror. I did look girly now. Shit, I said to myself.

'I am going to replait your hair too.' I put up no resistance. She was soon done.

'Come on then Alex.' She smiled her irresistible, innocently beguiling smile. The fact that she had reverted to my boy name reassured me.

We walked to the mall and browsed the shops, the women's wear, discussing looks and seeing what was in. She tried on outfits and I felt materials and looked at cut. I asked in the shops about jobs, but there were no opportunities, not even zero contracts going. A university town had a great surplus of young eager and intelligent casual labour. I was just one more student searching for employment.

Jacquie emerged from yet another changing room, giving back stuff to the attendant and shaking her head. 'Coffee and a bun. Are you bored with this.'

'No I like looking at the clothes.'

'Why haven't you tried any stuff on?'

'No money and actually not a lot of interest in clothes for myself and we have been stuck in women's wear.'

'Oh, OK, but you like looking at all the girl stuff; I mean for a boy, you have been really patient. You could try on a dress or some skirts and blouses, no one would remark.'

'What makes you think I want to?'

She just smirked, a Mona Lisa smile as though she knew some great secret no one else did.

'I am a fashion student. Just as you watch people for mannerisms etc., I look at clothes. I find clothes infinitely fascinating, that is why I readily agreed to come with you. This is my first time shopping with a girl, it has been an education.'

'I did think you might have come into the changing room with me and try something on. I thought you really enjoyed being a girl for the evening.'

I just blushed crimson and said nothing. I was thankful for the cold wind blowing up the Parade. This girl was too perceptive I thought and then, I changed my mind to imaginative, for I really had no intention of repeating what had gone on last night as much as I would like to.

She gripped my hand and looked into my face, a smile playing about in her eyes, lips moving infinitesimally. I knew she did not believe me but I reassured myself, I know who and what I am. Did I really? I was completely confused over my gender I realised in those moments when I could analyse myself dispassionately. Here I was out with a beautiful and vivacious girl and I wanted to be her or her girl friend. I did not think about sex with her. I did not think of forcing myself upon her, not even kissing her. Oh dear God! The pain was intense, I hated myself so. Was I mental? I am such a bloody mixed up failure.

We turned into a teahouse. After a short consultation, we ordered toasted teacakes with cinnamon butter, a pot of tea for two.

'So who am I out with anyway?' I asked.

'Me. Oh you really don't know me do you. Daddy is Sir Ralph Coles, the MD of UK Trucking. They have all those big red trucks with gold lettering. Grandfather was a country squire in Suffolk and we still own the estate, but a tenant farms it. I have two brothers who are both at Uni after going to Eton. I went to Cheltenham. Mum is on a few Quangos and secretary to the local hunt. We live in a large country house in Suffolk, Little Lettingham. I wanted to be an actress from the age of three. Daddy wavers between fearing for his baby girl, out among what he calls theatre people and, being proud of me. There, so now we know all about each other, except that you have a secret that you are not divulging.'

'What secret? I'm sure Gemma has told you all about the little nerd she grew up with at secondary school"

'Actually no. She never told me that you enjoyed cross dressing.'

'I don't.'

'Then why are you still wearing my knickers?'

I looked down at my waistband and sure enough the top of her knickers showed above the waist of the skinny jeans I was wearing.

I flushed. 'I don't know,' I said stupidly, then, 'I just sort of got out of bed and put jeans on. I was going to have a shower but I didn't get round to it.'

'So you wore my knickers all night long in bed!' She said looking cross.

'Please keep your voice down.'

She giggled. 'That's acting. I was good wasn't I? You were really worried that I was upset. Still, that is really very revealing. I saw what you hid in your drawer yesterday too.'

I said nothing. Bit my lip and looked at some of the tourist leaflets. She left the table and went to the door, I thought doing a runner and leaving me with the bill. She read a poster on the door. She turned and spoke to the girl at the till. She came away smiling.

I was so embarrassed. She obviously already knew my worst secret. I tried to ignore whatever she was doing, confused, stung, my inner secret revealed. I thought she chattered about her course. I drifted off, my thoughts elsewhere as she chatted on. She knows and I have no money, kept revolving round my brain.

'You are not listening.' She kicked me.

'Ouch Hey what? That really hurt.'

'Well, you didn't hear a word. There is a job going here.'

'Oh crikey. I better ask.'

'Come to the loos first.'

She grabbed my hand and led me downstairs. I was about to turn into the gents when she shook me and put her finger to her lips to be silent. She pushed the door to the ladies and looked inside. It was empty. She pulled me in. What now I thought? This crazy girl!

'This job is for a girl. It says assistant, but I spoke to the waitress while you were away in your little world. They really only employ girls. You could pass.'

'What apply as a girl, work here as a girl? You must be crazy. There are all sorts of problems. Anyway, I am not dragging up each day to come here and I am not free in the day.'

'This place does dinners. All day teas, evening dinners, that's when they want a waitress, a dinner waitress.'

'Yes, mmm let's see, slight problem, waitress, with little black mini and white apron, a girl not a boy. Then there are things like identity, national insurance number, tax etc.'

'Oh sure, look you can use any name you like. Just tell them you are Alexandra that the name is an error on your records. They are paying a good rate for evening work. Give it a go.'

'Even if the records are OK, I still have to get the job and I am a boy.'

'Look in the bloody mirror.'

I looked. Skinny jeans and a T, unisex wear these days. I examined my head. The pigtail, blonde and shining, eyebrows neat and tidy. Pale skin. I looked what I was I thought, a weedy youth, girl.

'I would never get away with it.'

'Let me tell you, you would. Gemma said last night, had she not known you and well, she would never have guessed last night that you were what's his name, like, oh yes, Alexander. Zandra is far nicer and pretty.'

'Did I really look that convincing?'

'Believe me honey chile,' she said lapsing into a Southern drawl, 'you look the silver dollar.'

'I need a job.'

'There you go. This is just super for you. I mean, five nights a week, every other weekend, six-thirty till eleven. The daygirl thinks they get ten pounds an hour at night, plus tips. She gets eight for days but because she works in a club two nights a week which pays better, she doesn't want this. Otherwise she says, she would do it. The boss is good.'

'So how am I going to apply?'

'Well as you are would do, but I think a little improvement is needed.'

Jacquie was already with the makeup. Eyebrows and mascara and a pale pink lipstick.

'You've done it again.'

'Wait, one more thing.' As if by magic and some wriggling, she pulled her bra from one sleeve. 'Get in the cubicle and get that on. Put some toilet tissue in the cups, it will make you so much more authentic.'

I did as she ordered. I emerged with bumps in the right place. We giggled and she squirted me with perfume.

'Go get 'em Zandra.'

'Zandra, right. I'll use that.'

We climbed the stairs and I went to the counter. "Can I apply for the evening job?' I said to the girl. She looked at me.

'I'll speak to the boss. Hold on a sec, take a seat there.'

She disappeared through a door. She reappeared and went back to her place at the counter. We waited.

After five minutes an Italian looking man came to the office door. He was about forty, not unattractive. He looked at me then did that thing Italian men do when summoning people, lifted his head.

I made my way to the office to find him already seated inside, even so, I knocked the glass on the open door.

'Come sit signorina.'

That sounded so strange and I thought I was going to be sick. My heart beat so fast I thought I was having a heart attack. I could hardly breathe. How would I ever speak?

'So you want to work.'

I nodded assent.

'Your name.' His accent was very Italian. I wondered in a flash if I crossed him, would the mafia be on my tail?

'Zandra, Zandra Gregson.'

'Nicea name. If you take this job, then it is five nights a week, every second weekend. You do not phone in with excuses, we must have staff. It is busy. Itsa hard work. You understand?'

'Yes sir,' I said, keeping my voice light.

'You need to dress right, whita blouse, black mini, black tights, nice patent shoes. Clean. We provide the aprons. You must be neat and tidy, make up your face. Varnisha the nails. We like a pretty girls and pretty smiling girls get tips. You must be polite to the customers, respond if they talk to you but you have to manage your station. All customers have the right to good service. You can do this?'

'Yes sir.' Oh god, what was I into now. It was so frightening. He could see how nervous I was.

'You are nervous, like a little rabbit. Sometimes that is good eh, you try harder. You want the work?'

'Yes sir, please.'

'Guiseppe, Zandra, my name is Guiseppe. We need your National Insurance number or your medical card when you come. You start tomorrow yes?'

"Yes Guiseppe.'

'Buono Zandra. Tomorrow, you dress properly.'

I left the office, face burning. Jacquie had disappeared. I went outside and found her there.

'Well Zandra?'

'Yeah, I got the job. Start tomorrow. What have I done?'

She giggled. 'You can do it. What is the money?'

'Five nights minimum, six-thirty till eleven, every other weekend. Ten pounds an hour plus tips, my own station.'

'Wow. We will have to put your rent up.'

'I have to get things and I have only about ten pounds. To be truthful, I have a twenty but I need some money for lunches. Will you help me?'

'Oh this will be fun. I'll lend you the money. Come on we have two hours. Lets go to H&M first. What do you need?'

'Black tights, black mini, white blouse, patent shoes with a heel, preferably not stilettos he says for his floorboards.'

'And a bra and knickers. Superb.'

'You are demented Jacquie.'

'You are the one cross dressing!'

'You are the one so gleeful. I need the money.'

'I am waiting for you to be truthful, with yourself if not me.'

Chapter 5.

We entered the store and Jacquie thrust a basket into my hand. We were soon in the underwear section and she was pulling knickers off the rail and throwing them in the basket. Then a couple of black and two white bras. I had no way of knowing if they were suitable. Next we picked up three different white blouses, really quite nice, little lace collars and pretty buttons and a couple of black minis that looked ridiculously short. Could I ever wear something like that?

I suddenly knew I wanted to try. It was an exciting prospect. I was very excited now. But a skirt that short, would I show more than I should? We entered the shoe section and browsed the racks, eventually selecting three pairs to try. Two were OK and stayed in the basket. We went to the changing room, taking in just the blouses and skirts. Jacquie came in with me.

'This is so embarrassing Jacquie. Are we mad?'

'You need money. There aren't that many jobs. A zero hours contract might mean you earn nothing. This is regular, plus tips. And you know, you'll fucking love it.'

I tried on the clothes in front of her appraising eyes. They glinted. The minis were fine but the blouses were tight. She vanished, to come back with the next size up. They proved fine if a tad over full.

'Good, now for your tights. This is such fun Zandra.' She surprised me again by a kiss on the cheek. We picked up tights on the way to the till. She paid. I was now worse off to the extent of sixty-three pounds.

'We need the loo,' she said and dragged me into the ladies and into a larger disabled toilet. 'OK. Get your kit on!'

'What now?'

'Yes now, get used to it.' She was tearing off labels. 'I'll have my bra back too.' I stripped and gave her the bra She handed me a new black one having torn off the label. I managed to put it on as she did. She seemed to have no modesty in front of me, baring her breasts towards me.

'Knickers,' she commanded and I replaced her pants with the black and lacy knickers. For once she remained quite serious. 'Tights.' I sat on the disabled seat and put the tights on. The blouse and skirt followed. Lastly the shoes.

'Done! My look at you. Those legs.' She repacked the bags with my cast off clothes and we left the cubicle. 'I just thought, you must have a bag and some sort of coat. 'New Look,' and she marched me along the mall and into the store. I tried on six coats before we found one she approved of and then allowed me to pick a bag, black patent, making sure it had the required compartments. It was beautiful. Was I going to be the owner of such a lovely item of girl attire? She paid, another thirty-seven pounds.

'Oh makeup. Come on, we just have time to get into Boots.'

There we made straight for the makeup section. She chose more items. I then owed her another thirty-six pounds.

'Phew. That's you then.' She stopped at a seat in the Mall. She pulled the coat and the bag from the plastic carrier. She ripped more labels off, using nail scissors to cut the hard nylon tags.

'Wear your coat it's cold out there.'

I put it on and buttoned it up. It had a round collar and flared out, reminiscent of the fifties styles. I simply loved it. She was already stuffing my bag with cosmetics. She arranged the strap over my shoulder and the black patent bag hung at my side. I looked at myself, using a shop window as a mirror. I was wet, I could feel that in my knickers. I realised that I loved myself as Zandra. I had never loved myself before. I examined myself minutely. Even I could not see Alex. Jacquie stood studying me. Her face was serious.

'Yes,' she said. 'I was right.'

'What about.'

'Everything. Look, you don't need to pay for all this. My present to you. You like the things don't you. Don't! Do not lie to me Zandie, or pretend. No fakery. I know you do like how you look as Zandra. I know you have some girlie stuff already and that is our secret. I just hope I have done the right thing.' She kissed my cheek and grabbed my hand. 'I feel so close to you. Home Zandra.'

She put her arm through mine, making me put the shoulder bag on my other side. She stopped and kissed my cheek, then continued walking holding my arm tightly.

'Are you OK?' She asked.

'I am sort of dazed. What have I done?'

'Well, too late now. Guiseppe expects and I have invested £136 in you. You can do it girlie.'

'I feel, I don't know, ashamed, but at the same time thrilled and excited.'

'Don't worry about it. Why ashamed? You are who you are. There is no human on this planet who is perfect. You are not a paedophile, a murderer, a thief, a philanderer even. Get it in perspective. Who are you harming? Here we are, home. Has it been an exciting day?'

'Exciting and terrifying. You are an exceptional girl.'

We entered. Sue and Gemma looked up and saw us, saw me and looked shocked. There was a boy with them. Somehow they controlled themselves.

'Hi.' Gemma said, 'This is Tim, Jacquie and Zandra.'

I managed a quick hi, turned with my bags and went up to my room. I put the bags on the floor and lay on the bed. I stayed there after I heard the door bang then heard raised voices.

A knock on my door and Gemma stood there.

'So what has she done to you now.'

'I'm dressed for work. I have a job, steady income. I had to be a girl to get it.'

'And you are OK with that.' She sat on the bed and took my hand.

'It seemed a solution.'

'OK. Cards on the table. No pride, no lies, no judgements.' She looked through the shopping bags, pulling each garment out laying things on the bed. 'The full kit, including bag and makeup. Do you like being Zandra?'

I felt my face turning pink. 'I, yes Gemma, actually, I do, I mean, it is not something I have done before in public, well not since a child, but I have always cross-dressed. It seemed a way to get some money and I haven't a bean. I can't explain, except to say, as Zandra I have left all Alexander's troubles behind. I feel free, if vulnerable. It's hard to explain except to say, I think meeting Jacqueline has been the best thing in my whole life. My world has burst into techni-colour after a period of sepia. Don't be angry with Jacqueline. She saw right into my soul.'

I found her arms around me, holding me tight and she kissed my cheek.

'Poor Zandra or Alex. Well I suppose I mustn't be hard on Jacquie then.'

'No, please don't be. Look if I had not wanted this then really, would I have been so malleable that she could persuade me against my will? You know me pretty well. I was strong enough to resist the school bullies.'

'OK. So have you thought this through? At college you are Alexander, at night Zandra. Can you continue like that?'

'I'm in fashion, we are all quite weird by your standards. Piercings, tattoos, weird dress. I am about the straightest person in my year. If I go all unisex, no one is going to turn a hair. Even makeup. Fashion is a weird world.'

'But at night, you have to be a convincing girl. You need work, particularly speaking, girls speak an octave higher at least, and from the throat not the stomach. Their voice rises up and down for emphasis and effect, men just drawl in monotones. Girls enunciate. And your body, your arms are too hairy and I can see a bit of stubble.

'Oh. You are freaking me.'

'Are you really going to do this?'

'Yes. I have to. Actually I want to.'

'You have to and want to? So this is not some aberration, a whim, a jolly jape? You want to go down this road, cross-dressing?'

'Yes. Please don't hate me?'

'Of course not.' There was a silence between us while she thought about it.

'Right then. OK. A friend has a laser machine which if used frequently, will get rid of the beard, but that will be permanent. Is that what you want? Just how far are you going to take this?'

'I don't know. For the time being, while I need money, I will lead a double life.'

'Yes but the voice, movement, stubble, that will not wait. I suppose, well, you do move like a girl anyway and you look like a girl. It is mainly speech and hair. Your arms are not that bad. Just your face.

'We will all help you. Jacquie and Sue will go to get a takeaway. Let's go down, pick what you want to eat from the menu and you and I will get things ready. After dinner, you will have some coaching. Tomorrow my dear friend Zandra, we are going to wax your body, so be prepared for pain. You will have to shave before you go to work in the evening, but you need to use the laser on your face and get rid of that hair permanently.

'Then there are other considerations.'

'What?'

'Well are you going to medicate, hormones. How far are you going? Or is this just an adventure?'

'An adventure.'

She looked into my face and said nothing, her face completely inscrutable. 'Truly?'

'It maybe more, I don't know.'

''I think you do. Downstairs Zandie. It's a good thing you came to us.'

I added my choice of Chinese food to the list.

Chapter 6.

When we all assembled downstairs, I found an atmosphere. Jacquie was tearful, Sue quietly sitting watching an early evening TV programme.

Gemma went to Jacquie. 'I'm sorry Jay, she's OK with it. I know how impulsive you are and I thought...No really I was not thinking. Zandie says she is strong enough to make up her own mind, and from our friendship at school, I know she is.'

'I'm actually here and you know, I am not really a 'she'.' I said. It was disconcerting to hear myself referred to as a girl. I mean I didn't really object, in fact I liked it, but it was so strange, they had already changed my sex.

'The hard truth is that I am a boy and I am only dressed as a girl. I am dressed like this for a purpose, to make some money to pay the rent. I am really Alexander Gregson girls.'

'Oh yes, that is so obvious, of course you are. Look how you are dressed, just as Alexander has dressed for the last eighteen years, since he came out of baby grows.'

I blushed. The sarcasm from Gemma quite hurt.

65

Sue looked up from her TV programme. 'Look, whoever you are or want to be, I am the neutral one here. You are Gemma's old friend. Jacquie has sort of taken you in hand as her project and if I may say, has done a terrific job converting you from, I don't know, what Gemma told us was a boy on the verge of a nervous breakdown into a pretty girl. I didn't see you before she got her hands on you, but I hear you looked terrible. Now look. When we came in from work last evening we found not Alexander but Zandra, pretty, in a mini, cooking tea. You spent the evening in the role and then today you walk in here looking even more girlie if possible, in a complete new outfit, right down to your black patent three-inch heels. Fucking boy? As far as I am concerned tomorrow, you can come in wearing jeans and a baseball cap, in Doc Martens and you will still be Zandra to me. I can't keep changing names and pronouns according to what you feel like wearing. So shut the fuck up Zandra and suck it up.'

She turned back to her TV programme and turned up the volume.

'I think that has told me. I'm sorry, call me whatever. What does it matter?'

'Are you staying dressed in your working gear? I think you should go and change. Come down again soon, wear whatever you want to Zandie. I have a feeling, and

Jacquie is convinced, you would rather be Zandra than Alexander. It doesn't matter, honest. You look better as a girl with some makeup than the pasty faced boy you were when I saw you six weeks ago at your parents funeral.'

I turned and left the room feeling as though I had somehow lost some of me. One thing was sure, I should not sit about in my work clothes all evening. I took off my blouse and hung it in the tallboy, the skirt too, using the little side loops to suspend it from the hanger. I stowed all the other new clothes in the tall boy. I smiled as I did so. I owned all these girl clothes. I caressed the little blouses, size twelve I saw. Well that was handy to know and I looked at the skirt labels, also size twelve. Shoes six and a half. I picked up the skinny jeans, caught sight of myself in the mirror, standing in panties and tights and a bra. I giggled. I put the skinnies on a hanger too and picked up the mini skirt and the top Jacquie had lent me and put them on. I checked my face in the mirror.

I picked up my handbag, my new handbag, my only handbag and found shadow and mascara. I used more eye shadow, dark grey and applied another two coats of mascara. I used the brighter of the two lipsticks, the one Jay had told me was better for evenings.

I turned in front of the mirror and made sure I was all together. I took a deep breath and opened the bedroom door and went down to the living room.

No one said anything. It was as if I was just one of the housemates. Surprisingly, it was Sue who patted the settee beside her, having forsaken her armchair for once, inviting me to sit with her. I did so. I was biting the inside of my cheek to maintain control. I knew that coming down like this, as Zandra I was making a definitive statement.

Jacquie said, 'We better go and get the food Sue. Do you want to come Zandie?'

'This girl is staying in,' I said.

Sue took my hand and shook it. Jacquie standing behind me ruffled my hair and kissed the top of my head. 'You better run a comb through your hair again now,' she laughed.

Gemma sitting in the other armchair came over and sat beside me. She took my hand and caressed the back with her thumb. "Looks like all the girls are home on a Saturday night then.'

Sue and Jay departed.

'Let's get things ready for when they return."

'Yes,' I said.

We put plates to warm and laid the table up with all the sauces and cutlery we thought we would need.

'You are all right with me like this?'

'Yes of course, if it makes you happy. I should have seen how you are long ago. I don't know how I missed it. I suppose we were so close I only saw what I expected to see.'

'And we will have a nice meal and you are OK with Jacquie.'

'Yes of course,' said Gemma.

'Thank you Gem. I am so lucky to have you as a friend.'

'No wonder you had a breakdown with this going on too. And after dinner, I am stripping Zandra's hair, arms and legs and anywhere else.'

It was going to be a merry evening.

Chapter 7.

After dinner, a very hot chicken Szechuan and Singapore fried noodle inside me, my three housemates set about my body. Sue settled for giving me a manicure while Gemma and Jay used hot wax on my legs, taking one each They worked up from the ankle applying the wax and stripping it off in one quick pull. It hurt, but not that much.

It became embarrassing when they reached my groin. They asked me to tuck tissues into my knicker legs and brought the wax right up to my nether regions. I closed my eyes and pretended that what so obviously resided in my panties, was not there. I had to spread my legs so they could do the inside of the thigh, then the bikini line. It was the most embarrassing moment of my life.

I was then turned and they did the backs. By that time Sue was working on my other hand. When my legs were done they did my arms and back of my hands, up to just above my elbows. By this time I had neat nails, nicely rounded, and to my surprise, finished in black and shiny nail varnish. That really turned me on and I was relieved to be prone on the bed, my penis safely out of view, squashed so it could not fill with blood. Damn thing. I was half turned so they could do each under arm.

They hadn't finished. They had a conference and decided that a bit of my face also needed attention, behind my ears and the sideburn area which was only bum fluff.

'All done.' Gemma said, at last, brightly. 'I'll get you a robe to put on then we can go down and watch TV together.' I waited while they departed. I had lain there still wearing the new bra and pants. I suddenly felt embarrassed, but it was a nice feeling. They were treating me exactly as if I was a girl. A week ago I was feeling desperate as though the climb out of the pit of despair was like crawling up hill in mud. A week ago I was cross-dressing in the woods, feeling a ruddy pervert, hating myself and punishing myself for it afterwards. Now I lay in recovery, in bra and pants, feeling elated, excited by what was happening to me and what I would have to do tomorrow, getting into my working gear and spending the evening as a waitress.

The door opened and Gemma entered with a robe. She threw it over me and as I sat up put one arm and then the other in the sleeves. It was palest blue and silky.

'Are you OK?' she asked tenderly.

'Mmm. Thank you. Do you think I am mad?'

'No. Why do you say that? I do want you to be honest though. You are putting up a token resistance to feminisation. Have you dreamt of this happening to you?'

I tried not to look at her, but she used a finger under my chin to raise my eyes to hers.

'Do I take that as a yes?'

I nodded.

'Often?'

'Quite a lot. Well, always.'

'All the time we were at school?'

'Always, from when I was tiny.'

'But you have never done anything about it?'

'No. I mean dad, he would have had a fit. Perhaps that would have been a good thing.'

'And did your mum not know. I mean she never said anything to me when we used to study together.'

'No, I never told her. I used to play in her cast offs as a kid, miles too big of course, then dad put his foot down. I longed for more girly clothes and, things, even envied the pencil case you used. I do wear girl's underwear. I self harm.'

'I never realised, that is why this has all been something of a shock and I blamed Jacquie for turning you, but it has always been there hasn't it?'

'Yes Gem. That is one reason I valued our friendship so much. It was as though being with another girl, some of you could rub off on me, a little of your femininity could enter my soul. At the same time it was quite frustrating. I wanted to be you, have your clothes and hair and adornments.'

'That is a bit of a relief, knowing it is not us that have turned you. OK, so no more pretence. I take it that when you are in the house, you will be Zandra.'

'I would like that.'

'And working too. That leaves college. I suggest you adopt an androgynous style, jeans are fine, the skinnier the better and tops which are female but bordering on masculine. We will try some different hairstyles. It's a good thing you have kept it long. So Zandra, we know where we are. You need to thank Jacquie for bringing you out. She is a super girl isn't she?'

I nodded. 'She is, you all are. Sue is very direct but truthful.'

'Sue always calls a spade a spade. I think we are going to like having Zandra here. It is going to be fun. Now we had a council when you were up here changing. We think you need some medical backup if you are serious, and before you admitted it, we thought you were anyway. As a start, you should make an appointment with the University Psychiatrists and Councillors section. They are there to help any student who has problems and no, don't say no, you obviously have an identity problem. You are doing this job. If they challenge your gender, you then have a defence, that you are gender non-specific or gender dysphoric and receiving treatment.'

'OK if that helps me stay within the law.'

'I think it will, and you do need help. I don't mean to change you but to help you achieve whatever you want to be. What I demand from you is that at least with us, you are totally honest, tell us what you feel, what you want.'

'Yes I promise. Everything is happening so fast. Three days ago I was a moping, grieving, nineteen year old boy. Now I am an honorary girl, eager to get on with my life.'

'I am really pleased to hear that. It is a relief that we now know the real you. So come down and watch a film. Tomorrow we are devoting to further feminising you.'

We watched a girlie film. I had never been into violent films, the worst I would watch, and I liked, were Indiana Jones. We watched 'Working Girl', one of their favourites. It was a beautiful evening.

As we went to bed, Jay said. 'We need to do more shopping, then, because you now need non-work clothes and some college gear that is more femme. No it's fine, I have the money, well it goes on the Visa which daddy pays, and he never queries it. We will have another shop, oh and as soon as you finish in college Monday, I am meeting you for a surprise. So shall we say Costa at four o'clock? And don't be late.'

Chapter 8.

Sunday morning. I was up first and I was to find this was the usual pattern. I showered and dressed, bra and knickers. I felt my smooth legs and arms. I looked in the mirror, and felt my chin. I was OK. I really would have to do something about that. I made my face, I thought not too badly. Then I looked more closely. I washed it off and started again. My hand shook as I used eyeliner. I stopped and tried again and this time my eyelid would not stop moving. I took deep breaths and tried to relax. I used the handle of the brush to practice moving something across my eyelid until I could do so without my lid fluttering or my hand shaking. I used the foundation dear Jacquie had selected.

At length I had my brows done to my satisfaction. I managed to do my eyeliner. Mascara was easier. I used the pale pink lipstick. I surveyed the result. It was much better. I looked OK, I did my hair, pulling it over to one side and fastening it with a clip Jay had used on me that first night before she did the plait.

I dressed in skinnies and one of my new blouses and added my work shoes. I had to get used to them and they had to get used to me before tonight. I would be on my feet for four and a half hours, well at least five because I had to walk there and back.

I was downstairs when Sue appeared. I had expected Jay or Gemma.

'Hi Zandie. Up early again. You look nice. Have you had breakfast?'

'No not yet. What are you having?'

'Oh coffee and toast. There's some of mum's marmalade too. Join me?'

'Mm sounds lovely.' I put the coffee machine on, topping up the water. Sue made the toast and I set the table. Gemma and Jacquie arrived. The kitchen was a bustle of activity until we were all sat and eating.

When we finished it was time for lessons. There are so many things girls, because of their anatomy and dress, do differently. They began with sitting and moved on to standing, pulling my torso into shape, shoulders back stomach in, hip tucked under. We moved to stationery stance, the weight on one leg and a hip thrust to the side, still keeping the upper body erect. Sue showed me how to put all my weight on one leg the other foot resting lightly on the toe, so lightly that the toe was not damaged.

I had to walk up and down the hall with a book on my head, chin up, proud, looking down my nose rather than through my brows. My hands had to be neat, thumbs tucked under which makes a hand look slimmer and clasped over my stomach or behind my back. They made me practice each move time and again laughing when I got it wrong, congratulating me when I got it right.

At twelve we moved to speech and I had an hour's speech therapy until I managed to maintain a fairly feminine tone. It was far from perfect, but they said, I had to stop feeling self-conscious, relax and Jacquie said, 'Act out of your skin. Don't be a blockhead, forget about Alex, you are not him and never have been, you are Zandra.' I started to get it. I had to leave all my inhibitions behind and think Zandra.

Tea was produced with some chocolate biscuits.

It was one thirty. 'Now we are all going to the Mall, shopping for Zandra, a complete set of clothes, chosen by us, paid for by my dad, but you will do the buying. Speaking to the shop girls will be good practice. I will change the pin on my card to something easy for you to remember and then change it back after. Let's go girls. Oh, and change out of those skinnies, not good for trying things on. So there is a lot on the list, three pairs of shoes, some girlie pumps, another six pairs of knickers and some black and white chemises. Three skirts, some girlie trousers, a couple of jumpers and three tops, a couple of cheapo bracelets, but nice and maybe a necklace.'

'That will cost a mint. I will never be able to repay that.'

'Daddy says his treat.' She smiled as we entered the Mall. She went to the cash point and changed the pin.

'OK here you are Zandra. The number for this afternoon is 1289. 'Right Primark first for nightie and PJs.'

We roved from shop to shop, all three thrusting clothes into my basket and taking it in turns to take me to the changing rooms, inspecting me with a critical eye. The store bags multiplied. There were a few extras, a makeup bag, a hat, hairbrush and a comb set, some conditioner for my hair, a scarf, the cheap jewellery, cheap but pretty and good for a late teen girl. These three knew so much about clothes and quality they could more or less tell at a glance, discarding things with a scowl. Most of my suggestions fell short or were totally ignored. I did get to choose my shoes. A pair with four inch stilettos and a T bar, some patent flats, and some little slippery pumps, flat and flexible in a blue flower pattern. 'Nice,' Sue said and I swelled with pride. They added a pack of black tights and some ten and fifteen denier non run ones.. Finally we were done. I had gone to the counter each time and paid, practising my female voice while one or other stood by my side and they gave a critique afterwards.

'Right quick teacake and tea.' Gemma said and led us into my place of work. I started to turn red. We entered shopping bags thrust before us, giggling and Jay poking me in the back with a finger. The place was half full and we found a table by the window.

Guiseppe came to the door of his office to see what the commotion was. He looked straight at me and nodded.

After tea we left. We had gone a few yards when Jay said she had forgotten something and returned to the café. We wandered towards home taking side streets that were a short cut. Jacquie caught us up.

When we reached home they all helped in removing labels and tags and helped put everything away. They laid out my outfit for the evening and to my surprise started pulling out my Alex gear, inspecting it and dropping some in a pile. On the pile went all my man pants and man socks, a tie and a shirt, a pair of jeans with no shape, and they were put in a plastic bag for the charity shop. These girls were just out of control. So was I.

At five-thirty I was commanded to go and shower and shout when I was in bra and knickers. Jacquie was going to do hair and makeup, making sure I looked as sexy as possible for a night as a waitress.

I loved the sensation of being done to, being passive while I was changed. I sat still, but kept smiling, loving the feel of this pampering by another's hand. It was just brilliant.

I could not contain myself. 'I love being a girl.' I said.

'I know. I could tell when I first played with your hair. I suspected then and when I dressed you, I knew. Good luck tonight. Now these are my last words of advice. You have to believe that you are Zandra, you have never been Alex, you don't even know him. Say who is Alex!'

'Who is Alex/" I said using my best girl voice.

'Again!'

I repeated.

'Try this, 'Table one, table two, table three!'

I did as bidden and she listened critically.

'OKish. Now how about, Good evening, have you decided?'

We went through other useful phrases and small talk.

'I really think you are starting to get it. I think you will do but it is not nearly perfection, don't forget to modulate and project and smile. When you ask if they have decided, you rise on the last syllable, 'ded?' Try!'

I tried.

'Yes miles better. Boys tend to go flat at the end of a sentence, girls really ask the question. Girls smile a lot, three or four times as much as boys. I suppose it is an old defence mechanism, from when we were apes and strong males could kill us with a blow. You are selling yourself as a sweet caring person. These customers are hopefully going to tip well. You have to please and nothing is too much trouble. Get dressed, time you were off.'

'Golly, I am going out there on my own.'

'Oh so you are little girl. You'll be OK. You can wear pumps there and take your heels in a bag. Yes? I think that is sensible or you will be limping home or walking in bare feet, both undesirable. Your coat and your bag, it will be cold when you finish. Your makeup is in your bag and a pack of hankies. Good. You are ready, your debut.'

They wished me luck and waved from the front step.

I tripped down the street in the pumps and walked through the now silent Mall and out past the market into the parade. Every step took me nearer what could be my 'guillotine'. My nerves nearly got the better of me. I wanted to run away and it was pride that got me to the door and my wish to please my friends by succeeding. I pushed open the door of the Old Kettle.

I reported to Guiseppe and found another Italian man with him. We were introduced. He was Gino the younger brother. They were in white shirts and black tie and looked after the wines and bills.

Gino showed me where to stow my things. I put on my heels and tied the apron I was given, making sure I tied a nice bow in the small of my back. Even that gave me a thrill. I was shown my tables, five in the back room, the first booking due at seven. They went through the menu, five starters, seven mains, and four sweets plus a selection of ices.

They taught me a few things about serving from the left and clearing from the right, making sure the condiments were on the table and full, providing a fresh jug of water, laying up and placing the starched napkins for the ladies. It seemed quite a lot to take in, but I had been to some posh places with mum and dad and it sort of came back, all the little actions one takes for granted as a customer.

I had just finished this minimum of training when other staff walked in and I was introduced. We gossiped and I found all but one of us were students. Luckily I'm the only one from the Creative Arts campus.

The first customers arrived and one of the girls showed me how to refer to the booking register to see which table they were on. The third people in were mine, a young girl and boy and their parents, a celebration of some sort. I picked up menus and asked them to follow me. I pulled the chairs out and helped the mother settle in, placed the menus and a wine list, and went away to fetch water in a glass pitcher. I returned and placed the water and asked if they would like some then upturned their glasses and filled them. I went to get a basket of bread and butter packs. By the time I had done that they had sorted out the menu.

I knew from my visits to the States with mum and dad, how professional the American waiters were. I introduced myself. "I am Zandra your waitress for tonight, if there is anything you want just let me know. Have you made a decision?' I remembered to smile and project as well as well as modulate.

They had and I took pad and pen from the pocket of my apron and took the order for starters and mains. I made a note of who was having what, making like a clock of the table.

I collected the menus and took the order to the kitchen. 'Ordering chef,' I called out, 'table eight, two garlic prawns, one soup, one melon. Two chicken maison, I sirloin rare and one sole meunière.'

The chef looked at me glaring. One of the girls said he always did that. I saw the sous chefs start to put the starters together.

I returned to the table and took the drinks order, a bottle of number fifteen. I put that on a ticket and gave that to Gino.

When I returned I had another table in. I settled them with menus and introduced myself as Gino was opening the wine for my first table. I saw him watching as I helped two ladies with their chairs and placed their napkins.

I served starters to my first table. Everything followed on. After that I had about thirty minutes until the next arrivals were due, a three on table five by the window looking out on the courtyard, used in summer but too cold in winter. I rushed back and forth with dishes, managing to place them in the right place without asking, making sure they had everything but trying not to be intrusive.

My first tables were well on the way, the first on mains, the second on starters when my three arrived and to my horror found it was my housemates. I blushed crimson.

I seated them as though I didn't know them and introduced myself. I helped them with napkins, shaking them out and handing to them. I brought them water and filled their glasses. I took their order and gave it to the chefs calling it out. I returned for the drinks order and gave that to Gino. I had another table after that, thirty minutes later and the last came at nine, a five. By that time the first had gone and I had the table cleared. My housemates were on their mains. I asked if there was anything else they required and apparently they were happy. They were, quite merry and that devil Jacquie tweaked my bottom.

Finally the five turned up and there were just my mates and the five left. Gemma ordered another bottle and coffee for later, but she would tell me when they wanted the coffee.

The five were on their starters, two bottles of wine on the table, candles lit and happy. It had all been quite hard work. As I took dirty dishes to the kitchen, Guiseppe signalled that he wanted to see me. I dumped the dirties with the porter and returned to the office.

'Zandra, you done a good job tonight, very good start. Easy, not too busy but you do well. Good tips so far. You tire yet?'

'A bit.'

'It will get easier. Go now, look after your customers.'

Phew so far so good. I fetched mains for the five and made sure they had enough wine. I ordered another bottle of red and refilled the water jug. My friends asked for their coffee and I found chocs for them too.

Next it was sweets for the five after I cleared their table. My feet were killing me. Ten forty-five and my friends still sat. The five had coffee, paid and departed. Jacquie asked for the bill and they paid. They sat on, saying they would walk me home.

I reported to Gino that I had cleared the tables and replaced the cloths. Just my friends were waiting for me. Two of the other waitresses had gone. Gino took me by the shoulder and steered me into the office and shut the door. Guiseppe turned in his swivel chair.

'You do good, you good girl. I like very much your work. Very professional. Where you learn?'

'In America Guiseppe.'

'Is very good. Your tips for tonight.' He gave me an envelope. 'I pay you wages after five days. You can go home now, bathe your feet.' He smiled and patted my backside. Gino kissed me on both cheeks and I blushed.

I discarded my apron throwing it in the linen basket. I collected my things, changing into my pumps, put on my lovely new coat and picked up my bag. I collected my friends and we walked home together.

We chatted about how it had gone and whether it had been fun. I said it had. I was elated. I had pulled it off.

Going through the Mall we linked arms and did a Madness walk. We giggled and some older people looked at us as though we were hooligans.

I was pretty tired and I was glad when we reached home. I opened the envelope. There was thirty-six pounds in there.

I went to my room stripped off and put on my new PJs, pink bottoms three quarter length, eau de nil top with lace around the bust, if only I had one. I removed my makeup and climbed into bed. I read my book for a few minutes and put the light out. I thought it had been the best day of my life, but now everyday seemed to be better than the one before.

Chapter 8.

Next day, Monday and it was Uni. I had not been for three months, I had missed six weeks of this term. I showered and washed my hair and blew it dry. I dressed in my new girlie jeans and a sweat shirt and some lightweight sand shoes. I looked androgynous enough. I still sported shiny black nails. Oh well, what the fuck I said. People could think what they liked.

I grabbed a piece of toast and a cup of tea. I was going to pick up my bag then remembered who I was supposed to be. Black polished nails and a patent handbag might be just a bit of a giveaway. I picked it up anyway and put it in my small backpack. I wore an old denim jacket and let myself out. I was in my art space just after nine and surveyed my work. I didn't like any of it. Somehow it all looked completely foreign and talentless. I tore down two designs. I had new ideas and I set to. I worked quickly, charcoal on parchment paper, inspired, feeling a new enthusiasm, full of ideas, designing what I would love to wear. By half past three, I had one new design with different aspects hanging and two more roughed out in front view. At three-thirty I packed up and made for the Mall to meet my mentor, Jay. She was waiting and we kissed in the French fashion.

I pulled my bag from my backpack and made my face while we waited for coffees. Jay watched an amused glint in her eye.

'OK, you will do my girlie girl. I have good news, a TV part, only small but my agent says the fee is in four figures. I think I may be getting somewhere.'

'That is super Jay, really good, I am so pleased for you. Jacquie, I want to say this while we are alone. I can't thank you enough for what you have done for me, really you have been an angel, my guardian angel.'

I had a tear in my eye, I felt so emotional, so beholden to her.

'You are a sweet girl Zandie. I hope you are going to be happy. Now come on, we have somewhere to go.' We collected up our things and walked down the Mall. She turned into a beauticians and I followed, thinking she was going to buy something. She gave her name and we were ushered into an inner room. An assistant came forward, pristine in a white overall with pink piping. 'Studs or rings?' she said.

'Studs, she would like studs.'

The girl was making marks on my lobes and I was shown a box of studs. I chose some with three millimetre crystals. Bang, each ear in turn and I had ear studs. We followed her to the till and Jay paid.

'Wow Jay, thank you. That will take some explaining.'

'I think the sooner you are out, the better, at uni too. Gemma has made an appointment for you on Friday with the psychiatrist in case you are challenged when out or at work. You have no work then until the following Wednesday. You should really think about being who you want to be at college. It will be a five minute wonder, but who cares.'

'This has all been sudden enough. A week ago I was a miserable youth, now I am a cross-dressing, I don't know what, with pierced ears and in knickers.' We had wandered through college grounds to the river. We perched on the bridge parapet and watched the activity below. Ducks paddled by, two swans moved serenely, like princesses in ball gowns.

'I hope I have not pushed you too quickly Zandra. Your brain needs time to catch up with your instincts and I caught you at a time when your ego was on the floor and probably your sexuality and sense of reality too. I am sorry, I have been an impulsive idiot playing with someone else's mind and body. I have been terrible"

'Don't say that. You made me see what has always been there, but with mum and particularly dad, I didn't dare show the real me. Dad was what I suppose was a man's man, someone other men looked up to, suave, manly, outgoing, liking a pint or a glass of red, rugby fan and cricketer. He knew about cars and treated women with courtesy but without consideration for what they wanted to do. A sissy for a son would have been the last thing he wanted. It was bad enough when he knew I wanted to do fashion design. Why not cars? He said, and why not? Except that I was fascinated by women and their clothes. When I came to college and started to design and make some things, I got this girl to model them, but I really wanted to wear them myself. It was only fear of ridicule and ostracism that made me refrain.'

'So perhaps I need not feel quite so guilty, but has it all been too much, too fast? Like last night, seeing you buzz round the Café in your heels, we could hardly believe you and you did such a good job, but it must have taken such a lot of nerve. I don't want to be responsible for a breakdown. If it is too much you must back off, go back to being Alex if that is easier for you.'

'Actually last night was super. I really enjoyed it. But it was not making money that thrilled, I enjoyed being Zandra, waitress, pretty and efficient and Guiseppe and

Gino saying they liked what I did. Me, the misfit in my black tights and patent heels. I made over thirty pounds just in tips, so I will be able to pay you back.'

'No, I told you, daddy has more money than he knows what to do with. It's good to help. So what now, where are we going with this?' We are all worried for you, that's why Gemma made the appointment with the psychiatrist. You will keep it won't you?'

'Yes, I will, I don't think I need counselling, I know where I want to go, but it will take time. In the meantime, I need advice which the psycho can probably give and I need security, in the unlikely event that something happens, like I get knocked down in the street and end in hospital. In the long run, I will need medical help won't I? I have looked at internet sites on trans people. I thought at first I was a trannie, a transvestite, but I don't think I am. It is not just the clothes, I want the body, breasts, curves and I don't want what I have down there.'

'OK. You have thought it out. I am relieved, So if you are not just a trannie, are you going all the way, a full sex change? If that is the case, then don't label yourself as a cross-dresser. That demeans what you are. I think you are really female, just your body is not right. I just brought you out didn't I? I thought for a time and especially Gemma did, that I had perverted you. Tell me it is not so?'

'It was always there, always has been since a small child. You saw those undies I attempted to hide when I unpacked.'

'Yes, well I saw something. So what now dear Zandra?'

'I am going to come out. I will wait until after this Friday appointment with the shrink. Monday I will go to college as Zandra, handbag over my shoulder, not hidden in my rucksack, makeup on and head held high. I am ready to challenge the world. People will either like me or won't, it is their problem. I have to be happy with who I am and these last four days, since you converted me, have been the happiest ever.'

'Ever?'

'Yes really. I grieve for mum, I can't get the imagined vision of her face as they went over the precipice, out of my mind. I grieve a bit for dad, but with them going, I am free to do what I want, what I am compelled to do. The awful loss, has given me freedom, for that brought me to you and you are so perceptive, you saw into my soul and you knew, you saw the girl inside, even though I was dressed as a scruffy male student.'

'It was somewhat intuitive, I think as soon as I saw you even before I saw a glimpse of undies as you put clothes away.'

She took my hand and we strolled the river-bank. She told me of her school and the pranks the girls pulled. I wish I had been there with her.

Chapter 9.

We walked home together, arm in arm, laughing and joking. I came across a fellow fashionista. He looked and I was not sure whether he recognised me or not, but I did not care. Soon everyone would know, and they would gossip and remark, but I was free, free of inhibitions, free to do as I felt the need to do, to be the person I had longed to be. My support network of Jay, Gemma and Sue had given me such confidence. It was a marvellous feeling, throwing off the shackles of my natal sex.

At home I busied myself changing into my work gear. If I was early Gino said, I could eat there before work, so that would save me time and expense.

I was greeted with real friendship this time, and chef put up a chicken dish for me, with some green beans and a few sauté potatoes. It was delicious. I looked at the bookings, just four tables tonight, Monday was usually their slowest day they said. My first table came in at seven fifteen, a party of six girls. Somehow that made me more nervous. Girls, I suppose, for their own self-preservation are more perceptive than men and well, boys notice hardly anything I found.

I went through my practised routine, my name is Zandra and I am your waitress for tonight, and they were soon laughing and joking with me. I got them on the wine and starters by the time the next table sat, three business men in their working suits and polished black leather shoes. They were soon having a flirt and I was coy, looking sideways at them, smiling, not giving smart cracks in return, maintaining good humoured tolerance even when one attempted to put an arm across my rump as I served his main. I did that thing girls do, rather than move their whole frame, they just move their hips, like a toreador facing a charging bull. I just said, Uh! Uh! and smiled. I liked the attention. It showed that I was attractive and that my disguise was complete. If it had not been they would most probably have hit me.

They asked if I was a student, and I told them I was, studying fashion and this was a way of paying the rent and being fed.

The evening progressed easily. I was much more relaxed and by just after ten, I was finished without feeling exhausted. I loved the work, meeting people, putting on the act, that nothing was too much trouble and it was a joy to serve such people.

Guiseppe called me and handed me another envelope. The girls had left a reasonable tip he said but the men had left thirty pounds for the 'charming waitress'. 'You see Zandra, first class service gets first class tips. Soon you will own this restaurant. Good girl.'

He rose and kissed me on both cheeks his stubble rasping against my skin. I stopped breathing, my first embrace from a man and I thrilled to it, even though I did not fancy him.

What I realised, but somehow had always known, was that a girl's or I should say, woman's life is so much more filled with affection and caring and even love of everything in this world for, people, babies, animals, colours of a sunset, clothes, curtains, even a clean and sparkling sink. Now I was in this new world, I realised that I had always been right to want it, crave for it. The dysphoria I had endured was not an aberration it was justified. My psyche could just not cope with a male world.

As I walked home I turned things over in my mind. Would I love men, I wondered? I never had as Alex. I had never had a crush on a boy, but now or when I have gone the whole way and had the right anatomy, would I love men or women?

At the moment, the person I was closest to was Jacquie. I adored her, she fascinated me and she above anyone had influenced me. I didn't know what would happen if I took hormones. How would that affect me?

Would they turn me on to men or had I already in that one embrace and innocent kiss from Guiseppe turned the corner?

The rest of the week went by uneventfully. By day I designed, four more designs. Thursday I was cutting out the patterns with help from our professor. She was interested in my change of direction and asked me into her office to discuss my backlog and whether I could make up the lost time. I said I thought I could.

She told me how sorry she was to hear of my loss. My unbearable grief had been understandable and they were all prepared to help me succeed.

She asked me about the ear studs and she said, 'I see traces of makeup. Do you know what you are doing?'

I blushed. I was going to lie then I thought, I can't, because I had promised myself that when I walked in on Monday, my handbag would be visible and I would be in mascara and whatever else I fancied, maybe not a mini but perhaps a more femme attire than now.

'Um, well, do you mind if I shut the door Professor.' I closed it.

'May I sit?' I sat opposite her, bit my lip and took a deep breath.

'I am living as a female, ever since I returned. I live with three girls who are all supportive and evenings I work as a waitress. I have to tell you now because next week I was going to out myself anyway, come in wearing more girly clothes and openly use makeup.'

'And you thought you would tell me when?'

'Tomorrow morning. In the afternoon I am seeing the psycho. I want to find out from her how to go about changing sex, well I think that's where I am heading.'

'You think or you know?' Are you just sugar coating for me here, making the change palatable. Be honest.'

'I am trying to be, that is why I am coming out. I have to be true to myself and express how I feel.'

'But you haven't answered my question. Are you changing your sex? There is no catch, I would just like to know.'

'It is hard to be honest, but yes. I hate what I am, I have always wanted to be female, from my first memories.'

'And you are certain? This is not just a reaction to your mother's death?'

'Oh no. I have always felt this way but buried it, mainly because of dad. Now I am free to be who I think I am.'

'And the waitressing? How is that?'

'I love it and I am good at it.'

'Where?'

'The Old Kettle.'

'So what are we to call you? Alex, Alexis, Alexandra?'

'The girls have christened me Zandra, like Rhodes.'

"Very apt. I like your new designs. I knew something catastrophic, no I mean significant had made a change in you when I strolled through last night and I popped in to see what you were up to. Well now Zandra, you must do what you feel is right. I will support you here and if there should be any nastiness, you are to tell me. I don't think there will be though do you?'

'No, I feel quite secure and I am so happy at the moment, expressing the real me at last, that I am much stronger. I can deal with any fun making or rudeness if there should be any.'

'Good. Let's finish off the pattern making. Then tomorrow you can start making up a design before your important meeting in the afternoon. I will write a note tonight, to take with you, just saying that you have my support and I recognise my duty of care.'

'Thank you professor. I'm glad you know.'

'There has been a deal of talk, others have noticed. Now I know how to deal with that.'

I told the girls that evening, before I went to work. They were hardly surprised.

I picked up my wages that evening, Nearly two hundred pounds plus a bumper forty two pounds in tips. In a week I had become top earner amongst the waitresses. On a table for two was my professor, with her, she whispered, unsuspecting husband. She too was very complimentary and so was he.

Chapter 10.

I arrived at the student psychiatric department with time to spare, dressed as Zandra, cobalt blue mini, black jumper, thick black tights and four inch heels. In my bag was a note of support from the girls and one from my prof.

I waited in a sunlit room in a new block having told the receptionist my name, in this case as booked by Gemma, Alex Gregson. Eventually a woman in her forties appeared and looking at me said, 'Alex Gregson.'

I rose from my chair and walked to her. She allowed me to pass into the room and pulled the door to, behind her.

She looked at me. 'I don't know why but I was expecting a boy. You don't look like him. So tell me, what's going on.'

'I am he, or should I say, was.'

'So tell me what has happened.'

'I always felt wrong as Alex but restrained myself while my parents were alive. It is quite a long story.'

'I have the time.'

I launched into my parents tragic death, loss of the house and living with my new housemates. I did not say that I was 'converted' by Jacquie, but said that they had helped me with makeup and clothes and I was now working as a waitress to pay the rent and keep myself. I said that from Monday I would attend college as Zandra, and intended to change all my records to my new name.

'So what can I do for you? I offer a talking therapy for those who are disturbed about something in their life, or a referral to a specialist. You seem to know where you are going, but still, I believe you might benefit talking it out. Is that what you are expecting from me?'

'No, well, not entirely. I sort of want your support, if anything should happen, if I were to, god forbid, be run over or arrested or something. And I need to have medical treatment, hormones etc., so I would have to see a specialist about that wouldn't I, or do you do that too? I am sorry, I don't really know what services you offer.'

'Yes, if you have gender dysphoria, then you need to go to a gender clinic, they specialise in cases like yours and if they are satisfied that you are convinced and convincing, they will offer hormone treatment and other treatments, like hair removal, voice therapy, fashion advice. They would eventually see you through surgery if that is the path you wish to tread. You mentioned arrest. There is no reason why you should be arrested is there? You are not involved in prostitution?'

'Oh god know. I was thinking more like drunk or a driving offence, and they are not connected either.'

'I am relieved to hear that. Well you are on my books now, so any question from the authorities regarding your sex, I can vouch for you and say you are under treatment. However, my advice is to be safe and stay away from trouble. Do you consider that you are stable?'

'Oh I am now. A fortnight ago, I was anything but. I was a really unhappy bunny. Now, yes, I am content and I feel strong too.'

'Good. Oh you have some letters for me.'

I gave her the two envelopes. And she opened and read them.

'Well you seem to have a good support network. Your professor has seen you working as a girl and was impressed. She says you intend coming out in your course from Monday and is willing to allow that, not that she really has a choice.

'Your flatmates say you are just one of them and they are very fond of you but worried that you are not so far having treatment or official support.

'It all looks very good. You seem balanced, you look, divine. I will give you a couple of my cards so that if for any reason you are in trouble, police or not, you can contact me to get you out of a cell.' She laughed. 'My advice is, stay out of the hands of the police, they are more PC than they used to be, but still have a way to go. In the meantime, I think you should see your GP and ask him to send you to the gender clinic. If for any reason you have difficulty, get in touch. You are not alone, but I think you know that. I want you to make an appointment for a month's time. I would like to monitor your progress Zandra.'

I was dismissed. I made another appointment as she had asked. I went immediately to the GPs surgery where I asked for an emergency appointment. The receptionist wanted to know the reason and I just said it was personal and the University psychologist had sent me. That moved her, she spun off her chair and dialled a number. She spoke in hushed terms and asked me to take a seat.

I waited and at length I was summoned into the consulting room of Dr Mason. I had never seen him before. I found he was a young man in his thirties.

He was looking at his computer screen.

'I was expecting a young man. Is there something wrong with our records? I see you have not been to us before.'

'My name is Alex Gregson, officially male. I am now living as a female and working as one as well as attending Uni as a girl from next Monday. I am just coming out.'

"Oh I see. This is a first for me. And your visit today is for what reason?'

'I need to start hormone treatment and I understand if I am to get that, then I need to go to the Gender Clinic in London.'

'Right, well I am certainly out of my depth, but referring you on is no problem and I take it, given how you look, fairly urgent? OK. I will get a letter off and then they will contact you direct. While you are here, I will just check you over. Would you hop on the scales?'

He checked weight, heart rate and listened to my chest. I blushed when I raised my top and revealed a black bra that contained no breasts.

'I think we will take some blood too while you are here.' He typed information into the computer and the printer started to whirr. It produced a form.

'I am writing to the clinic which I understand is in London. In the meantime give this to reception and they will find someone to take some blood. Good luck to you, but somehow, I don't think you will need it.'

I returned to reception. I sat and waited and a nurse called my name and I soon gave some blood. It was quite painless.

I had set the wheels in motion on a voyage to a new life. It had all happened in a week, mostly thanks to Jay and her wealthy father. I had offered to pay some of my debt, now nearly four hundred pounds, but she had refused, becoming quite annoyed when I pressed. She was a brilliant girl.

On the weekend we sought of did our own thing on Saturday. Sue and Gemma worked all Saturday. Jacquie was busy with her own stuff in the morning and reappeared at two.

'What are you doing?" She asked when she came in and found me lounging with a book.

'Nothing really.'

'Do you fancy a run out in your car? I know somewhere where we can see the river and have toast and tea, then get back and cook for the girls. How about it?'

'Yes great plan. I'll just go and tart a bit."

'I'll come and watch, make sure you are doing it right.'

'Oh by the way Jay, a parcel came for you. I put it on your bed.'

She disappeared into her room and I heard the sound of tearing paper. She reappeared, her face full of humour, impish. 'Look what I have for you,' she said.

'What the devil?'

'Breasts, to put in your bra, size B. It will just look better.' She unbuttoned my blouse and inserted them in my bra. I told her about the GP yesterday.

'OMG, that must have been so embarrassing for you. How were you to know that he would sound your chest. I am glad you are taking action yourself. And you haven't told me about the shrink either.'

I told her of all that happened.

'You are much braver than I ever thought a week ago. So really serious now. And you are totally sure? I just feel this great responsibility.'

'I told you, you were merely the catalyst, I always felt like this, I was just frightened to express it. And I am going in on Monday as Zandra, I think the Prof is preparing the ground. It will be a relief to be Zandra all the time. This thing is just snowballing and I am glad.'

She was buttoning my blouse. She looked directly into my eyes and kissed me on the lips. 'The sister I never had,' she said. I blushed red hot.

I touched up my lips grabbed a jacket and my bag, my handbag, I loved it, loved having this emblem of femininity.

We drove out of town deep into the countryside and ended up by the river, with the chalk hills behind us and a sizable stretch of river before us in front of the pub. There were a number of cars and a few walkers with dogs. We entered and found a table overlooking the river. Afternoon sun streamed in the window.

'Your hair glows in the sun,' she said, and I glowed within too at this remark. She ordered for us.

'So little cherub, Monday, the big reveal. Wow, I wish I could be with you. Look meet lunchtime at the cafeteria, and you can tell me all about it. When do you work again?

'Wednesday through Sunday, five days and then three days off.'

'And you are enjoying it still?'

'It's real fun, yes, hard work but really lovely and I'm good at it. I make nearly as much in tips as pay.'

We lazed away the afternoon, gossiping, talking about our families, difficult for me still. I told about my cat and dog being rehomed. I just hoped they were OK, but there was really nothing I could do for them. We returned in time to make dinner.

Chapter 11.

Sunday we all lunched in a pub by the river. Life had never been so good and I said so. I had never realised the camaraderie of girls. I thought it was men that clubbed, joked and yarned, but we four had a gorgeous time, yarning and gossiping, laughing at silly jokes.

When we returned home, I asked what I should wear for college in the morning.

'I suggest eyeliner and mascara, a touch of lippy.' Gemma suggested. 'How would you like your hair? We could put some waves in or crimp it, that would be really girly but not too elaborate.'

'Yes that would work and you could still catch it back in a ribbon on your neck.'

'I think you should make a statement over your dress. If you are a girl, then nothing looks better than dark tights and those suede effect shoes. You have that red mini and you have a black sweater with that shiny inter weave. It would be really effective.'

'I like it. Thanks girls. So no concessions then?'

'Oh no. No why should you, if you are out girl, then you are out, and the lovelier, more femme you look the better too.'

Monday morning came quickly and as planned I dressed in the red mini, black top with a little cream blouse with Peter Pan collar under it, black tights and patent shoes. The girls had all risen early to see me off and sat on my bed, making sure I was pristine. Jay touched up my make up, emphasising my eyes even more. Gemma crimped my hair and tied it back with a red ribbon letting it fall loosely at the sides. I felt I had been prepared for something great, like a wedding day, or a prize giving. I was very emotional. I loved my reflection and I loved these girls.

'Now girl, go get 'em,' Sue said.

I wore my nice flared topcoat as the morning was quite cool. My patent bag slung over my shoulder and backpack in my other hand, I was escorted to the front door by my team and kissed by each. I felt like a child going off to first day at big school. These girls were pure gold and I told them so.

I set off on the half-mile walk to the Creative Arts block.

I swung along in small strides in the three-inch block heels, enjoying the air on my legs, and the touch of skirt on my thighs. The ponytail bobbed with each step. I knew I looked good. My bag on my shoulder further emphasised my femininity. It was liberating, I felt free at last, able to show the world the real me.

I walked in the door and showed my pass, the guard did not even look at it otherwise he might have noticed the difference.

I took the stairs to the first floor, my heels clacking on the concrete steps and entered the long corridor past Jewellery to Fashion.

I pushed through the double doors and found Hugh, one of the senior fashionistas, there on his mobile, I just heard him say, 'here now.'

I walked down the corridor to my little studio. Before I reached that, I had to pass the large cutting room that was used for any meetings. Surprisingly I found it full of students, stood backs to me, around the one large long cutting table. I wondered what was going on.

Prof stood in my way. She clapped her hands and all the fashionistas turned and clapped. I blushed crimson and did a little pirouette and curtsey, luckily without falling off my heels. The café must have been good practice.

'Thank you everybody,' I said. 'You have made me so happy.' I felt tears welling in my eyes and I almost ran from the room. I made for my studio and found a hankie. I was dabbing my eyes when Charlotte entered, short dark red hair, nose stud and tattoos on her arms. She wore jeans always, with black Doc Martens.

'You OK kid?' she asked.

'Yes Charlie, thank you,' I snivelled, 'never better.' I was laugh crying.

'Well you look the real deal, I'd take you out. When are you free?'

'Oh Charlie, now that would be an experience, wouldn't it?'

'You know what my dad always said, and he was as hetero as a male elephant in musth, don't knock it till you tried it. Anyway, it was not entirely a surprise, we were speculating all last week.'

'Oh, I didn't think I was that obvious.'

'You have always been obvious, dubious, well, we just thought you an effeminate gay. So you aim to join the sisterhood?'

'Always thought of myself as a girl, wanted to have dresses. I hid my feelings until I came back. My parents' death has set me free. I live with three girls and they have helped me.'

'Well good luck Zandra and if you ever feel like a walk on the dark side, see me.' She laughed and left.

All day various members came and wished me well. Some didn't, but I did not expect to win everyone over.

My work progressed and my designs took shape. Having looked at them, Prof had said I could make up three of the six designs, one I had already cut out. She assisted in making patterns for the other two.

I started sewing the first, made to my own measurements. I would model them myself. This was a cocktail dress, four inches above the knee, a reduced tutu skirt and a bodice with wide shoulder bands, and a plunging back. I was making it in dark emerald silk dupion, studded with crystals.

It took me the rest of the week. There were layers of tulle in contrasting eau de nil, the bodice had to be supported by bones that had to be carefully positioned in pockets and the whole bodice stiffened so it would stand on its own. I spent four days sewing and swearing. The hardest part was positioning the waist to sit exactly.

Charlotte assisted me. By Friday I was wearing it. I hung it in the dress cupboard in a plastic cover.

The café was going well. Friday and Saturday were really busy, flat out all evening, six tables with relays for second sittings. It was mad but it mostly went well, at least I had no complaints, though one table did sit for twenty minutes between starter and main. I apologised and brought them another bottle of wine, which I told Gino I would pay for. He said not to worry; in this case they would cover it because part of the trouble was a back up in the kitchen.

Each week I managed to put together another dress, concentrating as Prof said, on workmanship. The end of year show, whether we were graduating or not, was viewed by rag trade companies looking for talent. The finish was almost as important as the design, I learnt.

Other students became interested, especially when I started to model them myself. Mostly they were complimentary, one or two just smiled. Geoff Ainsley said quietly, 'Perhaps I should put on a fucking dress.'

I received the appointment to go to London Gender Clinic two weeks after my visit to the GP. The date was Tuesday the following week.

I told the girls and immediately Jacquie asked to come with me. 'Of course,' I said, 'I'd love you to, but it is my treat. I pay for your ticket and I'll take you for a meal.'

'If you like, but lunch will be on me, well on Daddy. He works in the city and he will take us to lunch.'

'Oh meet your father? Does he know.....?

'About you? No, I don't really talk about my housemates and certainly not our little dressmaker, other than the day to day.'

Gemma had met a boy and he took up three nights a week. Sue had several clubs she belonged to, tennis and rowing and athletics so they were both busy. Jacquie was still free, mostly. She had been away for a week doing a TV show, a small part with ten lines of diction in two scenes. Now she was back and devoting time to me. I was pleased, for of all three housemates, she was the driving force behind me. She alone seemed to understand me completely whereas Gemma and Sue were supportive but I felt, and I have developed a heightened sixth sense, that they did not fully understand me.

Perhaps it was their different backgrounds. Jacquie was rich; her grandfather was Sir Robert Coles, owner of a large Norfolk estate. Her father, although in an artisan industry like transport, had also gone to Eton. She went to

Cheltenham where nothing much mattered except good manners and money, not necessarily where the money came from. Her classmates might have been daughters of pop stars or Earls, so she was used to diverse personalities.

Gemma and I had gone to what was thought to be a good comp, Dad believing that a boy worth anything would rise to the top anyway. But of course, Gemma had known me as a boy, however weird I may have been, so my change took some getting used to.

Sue had gone to an academy. In both schools it was convention that was valued. I was anything but conventional but Sue was the straightforward one. She took everything at face value and as long as everything was fine in her world she did not bother about what other people did. It was truly live and let live. She had a relaxed attitude to life. So with me, as soon as she had sorted me out regarding name and sex, I seemed just to be Zandra.

Now it was Jay who really looked after me and pressed me forward, analysing my mannerisms and dress, educating me in decorum. I don't mean to say that I was a complete slob without manners, but having been brought up as a boy and my only real friend having been Gemma, there was a lot to learn, especially small things, like how to wear a silk scarf or a thicker scarf, how to arrive in a restaurant and take a seat at a table, how to get in an out of a car without showing the world, as she put it with a laugh, 'what you had for breakfast'. I had to learn even, how to accept a door being held open for me as though it is a natural courtesy. You may think the latter easy but when one has been left to fend for oneself previously, it is difficult to accept with good manners.

So I was doubly pleased to have her company to London and the invitation to meet her father, the son of a baronet. That should not have impressed in this age of dumbing down, of denigrating any class difference, of lowering all behaviour to the lowest common denominator. Her grandfather had been a Governor of a West African colony and had faced down an uprising, unarmed except for his staff of office and a plumed hat. I admired that. What I dislike is the self serving, financiers, bankers, pop stars and actors being given such honours.

Jacquie, as we called her, was always Jacqueline at home she said and I would try to remember.

Chapter 12.

I drove to Epping with Jay and we arrived just in time to get one of the last parking spots at the Underground station. I bought the returns to Barons Court.

My heart started to beat more quickly as we walked through the cemetery to Fulham Road. We entered a door after using the intercom and mounted the stairs. I wondered what I would find on arrival. There were five or six people waiting already, some distinctly weird and some really old. I wondered they had delayed the change for so many years. There were a number of really weirdly dressed older people and I certainly didn't want to be in the same category.

There was one young girl there, about seventeen who could not stop preening herself. Her poor mother looked distinctly embarrassed. My heart went out to them both.

I presented my letter to a busy clerk and we were asked to take a seat. Surprisingly I was called in quite quickly. Jay asked if I wanted her to come and I said I would like her to, if she wished.

We entered and were asked to sit. I explained that Jay was a close friend.

'So you are living and dressing as a female and attending university. What course?'

'Fashion, I am what they call on campus, a fashionista.'

'And how long have you been cross-dressed?"

'Well permanently for five weeks, but virtually all my life in secret.'

'And why do you do this unnatural action?'

'Oh that is a surprise question. Oh I see, because I feel I should have been a girl, I feel like a girl and identify with the female sex. I have always dreamed of being a girl.'

'That is all I was asking. There are no catch questions. You have always felt this way? You dreamt of what? Being a girl or being changed?'

'Yes, both.'

'And why has this suddenly become so important that you have come out and come to see me?'

'My parents were killed in a car crash four months ago. Father was in debt and I have found myself with no parents, no financial support and no inhibitions, no one restraining me, no one to shock or disappoint. It was time for me to become the person I always wanted to be.'

'But if your home still existed, would you be doing this?'

'Oh I am certain I would be, but it might have taken longer to come out. Father was a man's man, he expected me to be much more manly than I ever have been. But this desire, this belief in myself as a female, is so strong that in the end I would have had to declare myself.'

'And this young lady is here why.'

'She is my friend and has assisted me a great deal to become as I am now.'

'You are at university. You say you now have no financial support, how do you live.'

'I work five nights a week as a waitress.'

'Successfully?'

'Oh yes, I get more tips than the other girls and my bosses think, well, they are very complimentary.'

'And what do you want me to do?'

'I would like to have hormone treatment and eventually surgery.'

'You are certain about this?'

'Oh yes. In spite of the grief over my parents sudden death that sent me into a spin for three months, I have come out of it into a sunlit world of being a girl.'

He smiled for the first time. He sat examining me. It was disconcerting.

He turned to Jacqueline. 'How would you assess your friend?'

'Every inch a girl. Sweet, hard working, interested in her girl friends, considerate, what the Italians call simpatico and the French sympathique. We live in a house of four girls, us and two others. She is just one of four.'

'My purpose is to be sure you are convinced and convincing, to assist you in your desire, whatever that may be. If you change your mind, there is no shame in that. If you want to transition and are firm in that resolve, then I am here to assist you. A word of warning though, this period before surgery is for you to be certain. You cannot have everything put back as it was after surgery, in other words, if you go through any sex change surgery, you will never be a proper man again.'

'Thank goodness.'

'You seem very certain. Tell me more. Have you been depressed for example?'

'Moments of despair, I mean dysphoria, hopelessness. Having a life that was meaningless. I don't think I was ever suicidal, but after cross dressing I would sometimes, well often, self-harm.'

'And now?'

'I love my new life. I feel it has a meaning and a future.'

He started writing. He held out a prescription. 'Give this to your GP. You will have three drugs, two to kill the nasty male hormones and oestrogen for feminine development. I want to see you initially in six weeks, thereafter every three months, to monitor your mental state. Some turn back after the initial euphoria. In six weeks, if you are still convinced, I will put you on the surgical list. You will have a two-year wait. In that time you may turn back or not. It is entirely up to you.'

'Thank you.'

'You may go. Make an appointment for six weeks time.'

We left. I made an appointment. I felt absolutely elated. I waited until we were on the landing and jumped up and down. I skipped down the stairs. 'I'm on my way.'

I grabbed Jay and kissed her. 'Thank you for everything.'

'Come down, you will explode. We are meeting daddy in the Duck and Waffle. I hope you are going to be sane by then.'

Chapter 13.

We took the Tube to Liverpool Street and walked to Bishopsgate. We entered the building and were directed to the glass lift that whisked us to the fortieth floor. I thought we were going to a city pub not a posh restaurant in the sky.

I felt vertigo, almost sick as the ground receded. I was glad to arrive at the restaurant floor and get out on what felt to be more like solid ground. I was still conscious that we were so high we could see easily across the top of the Gherkin building to the Shard on the South Bank.

A gentleman arose from his leather armchair as we entered and Jay's father came to clasp her to his chest and kiss her tenderly.

'My favourite daughter,' he explained to me.

'Your only daughter,' she retorted.

'Well as far as you know.' He said saucily.

'And you are Zandra. I have heard a lot about you, a talented dress designer and a waitress I hear.'

'I am certainly a waitress, whether a talented designer, others will have to decide.'

'I am sure if my daughter says you are talented then you are.' He turned to Jay. 'Your mother hoped to come but she has an emergency meeting of some committee or other. Anyway, we are here, forty floors up, the highest restaurant in London.'

'I'm sure it is fabulous but I hated the lift.'

'Oh I am sorry about that, maybe more a bit of a boy thing. My sons love it. Anyway the food is good, so I hope you girls are going to eat and not worry about your lovely figures.'

'And I might learn a few waiting tips,' I said.

'A professional observation. So you can tell me, what is my darling daughter getting up to at university.'

'Nothing bad I can tell you. She seems to be getting known as an actress and personally she has been a terrific friend and encouragement to me since I joined the household.'

'A staunch ally, Jacqueline. A rather large Visa account landed on my desk, for all sorts of clothing.'

'Yes daddy, I just needed quite a lot of new things.'

'Well you know your allowance, try to keep within in it.'

'Yes Daddy but as an actress I do have to look right and very often I don't spend all my allowance.'

'Oh yes, I saw you in that advert for chocolate. You looked really good. I expect there was a fee, will I receive a percentage Jacqueline?'

'Daddy you are impossible. You put on this act of being so mean and we all know you are not, and daddy, you know you are well off.'

'I shan't be if you keep spending. Your brothers have about three shirts between them. Anyway, I was very proud seeing you on the screen. And you have been in a TV production too. I'm looking forward to that. I suppose when you are famous, you will pay back all my investment, keep your mother and I in old age.'

'Daddy, don't pretend you are hard up, and don't make out you are mean.'

He took her hand and kissed it.

We ordered or rather, I let him order for me.

The food was terrific and the waiting staff efficient without being obsequious, but they weren't friendly. Our clientele at the café looked for friendliness and efficiency without being intrusive.

I ate well. I kept thinking of the prescription safely stowed in my bag and how I hoped the drugs would change my body and stop any further depredations by male hormones. I could not wait to present it to my new GP. I excused myself, walking to the foyer, where I called the surgery and made an emergency appointment for next morning.

I returned to the table. Almost immediately the main course was served, crevettes in a garlic and parsley sauce with minute amounts of artistically positioned veg and a small tower of rice. A streak of tomato and paprika sauce finished the artistic masterpiece. Oh yes it was all delicious but it would not have sustained a bricklayer nor for that matter the woman we saw sweeping the foyer on the ground floor. The sweet of what was described as warm chocolate mouse and almond ice cream was absolutely wonderful. I just could have wished for twice as much ice cream.

'Now while you were away, Zandra, my daughter was saying you have nowhere to holiday. I saw your father race once, he did OK. I am sorry for your loss. Would you like to stay with us for your three-week break? Jacqueline would love your company, and you have your car, so you would not be a prisoner, and you might meet some people who would eventually become customers for your frocks.

'Oh, thank you so much. Really, I mean it seems such an imposition. I was thinking I would have to go to my aunt only there are difficulties there at the moment. Truly Jay, do you really want me to stay with you?'

'Of course, you are my project.'

'Good that is settled. It will be nice for her to have another girl to be with. Do you ride?'

'Horseback?'

'Yes. We have a couple of horses that always need exercise.'

'I have not ridden since I was eight. I could try.'

'That's the spirit. So you will bring our daughter home in your car?'

'Yes of course.'

'Good, save me the trouble and the fuel.' His phone lying on the table started to jump about. He picked it up and listened. 'Oh I will be back in about twenty minutes. Entertaining two fabulous girls, yes my daughter and her friend Zandra, no not Rhodes, but close.' He put the phone down and signalled for the bill. 'Well girls, duty calls, have to pay your clothes bills somehow. We'll go down together.'

We parted on the 6th his office floor. He kissed us both.

'Jacqueline,' I said as we walked to the Liverpool Street tube, 'thanks. Do you really want me to stay for the whole holiday?'

'Why, don't you want to?'

'I would love to but I don't want to be your burden.'

'Look I want you to. Anyway, you haven't told your aunt yet have you?'

'No, I must, during this holiday. I will have to see them.'

'Well I insist on coming with you when you do. They live not far from us anyway.'

'Oh gosh. It's going to be awful.'

'I suggest you phone them first.'

'Or write a letter? I could say things coherently in a letter. Speaking on the phone, I just might muck it up.' I said trying to escape.

'Write down what you want to say and then phone. When did you last talk to your Aunt?'

'Two weeks ago.'

'And you gave no hint then?'

'No I just said everything was fine, I was feeling much better and how much I enjoyed living with you all. I said I was just one of you. That might have told her but I wouldn't think so.'

'Nor would I. Now you are definitely on your way, you must tell them. She will then put it round the rest of the family. These things spread like wildfire.'

'Oh damn. Yes, I must, after all she was mum's sister and she has been very decent.'

'Tonight when you get home.'

'Jacqueline, why do you put up with me?'

We had arrived at the entrance to the station. She caught my sleeve and swung me round to face her. We stood there in that busy street in the middle of the City, spring sunshine streaming down onto our sunny side of the street. I breathed in the scent of the City, not unpleasant, but distinctive, exhaust mixed with dust and I suppose, the smell of humans. Her eyes were piercing, blue with green flecks, the colour in this strong light so brilliant, light glinting in her hair.

'Don't you know?'

'No, why are you so good to me?'

'I love you, you dumb klutz. No not like that, like a sister. You are the sister I never had. Now come on, let's get that train to Epping.'

'One more thing. Your dad does he know? You said he didn't.'

'Oh yes, you noticed. Yes, I do tell my family most everything. I'm sorry but they are cool. Do you mind?'

'No, somehow I don't. He was quite sweet and I suspect he knew who the all the clothes were for.'

'I guess, but never mind. You had to have them, I, well he has the money. Honestly he doesn't really mind. Mummy is simply dying to meet you.'

We arrived home by five-thirty, time enough for me to get my glad rags on for the evening shift at the Kettle. I had to tell the two Gs that their best waitress was taking off for three weeks. I hoped they would keep a job for me.

Chapter 14.

I spoke to Guiseppe as soon as I arrived at work. He was upset.

'But you knew Guiseppe, that I am a student and in the holidays, students go home.'

'I cannot lose you for four weeks young lady. It is too much.'

Gino entered the office and they spoke Italian. They seemed to go on for ages and I felt like a spare part. At one time it was so voluble that I thought they were arguing with each other, their voices rising in strength. I tried to leave to look at the bookings while they argued, but Guiseppe seized my hand, anchoring me in the small office between these two large men.

'Two and a half.' Gino said finally.

'Si, two and a half week holiday, then you come back, or we find new person.'

I thought quickly. I would not get another job that paid so well and probably Jacqueline's family would be fed up with me by then. If the worst came to the worst I could drive the fifty miles from her home to work and back afterwards.

'Three weeks, but you have to feed me each night.'

'You come here six o'clock, evening, and itsa deal.' He put his hand out. I shook his hand and Gino grabbed me and kissed me.

'Now there is small trouble. You give me identity for Alex Gregson. You are not Alex Gregson, you are not him.'

'I used to be,' I said.

They looked at each other and then the Italian jabbering started again. It seemed it would never stop and I was penned between them, Guiseppe sitting in his old wooden swing chair at the oak desk with papers spewing from every cubby hole, Gino standing in the doorway, a smirk on his face.

'No, non possibile.' Guiseppe thrust back and rose from his desk, the chair skittling across the floor.

'Si, possibile. Lo sono un transessuale.' I said, an Italian phrase I had learned deliberately in case such an occasion arose. 'Ero un ragazzo, ora sono una ragazza.'

They looked at each other and then burst out laughing. I didn't know what the hell was going on. Then I found Guiseppe's arm around me. He took my hand and kissed it, Gino kissed me on the cheek.

'Is that OK?' I asked in alarm.

'Is OK Miss Zandra. Go prepare now.'

I did as told. That was that then. It was best they knew. I returned, 'It is our secret, yes?'

'Si si, our secret.' They said. They were still chuckling. I didn't see the joke.

I told Jay next day that I had three weeks holiday when term ended, and then I would return.

'I may come back too.' she said.

'Why?'

'Oh just because, well for one thing, the theatre group are looking at a new play and to be honest, I would like to be here for you. We can be together during the day, have days out, perhaps go to London for a couple of shows on your days off.'

'Oh Jacqueline, do you mean that?'

'Of course. I told you, we are sisters. Anyway, how are those dresses doing? Have you finished?'

'Sewing pearls and crystals on the wedding dress. Then I am done.'

'I would like to see them.'

'Come tomorrow about four, then I can show you and we can walk home together.'

'Deal.'

I was still sewing pearls when Jay arrived in the afternoon. I showed her the wedding dress then put it on a dummy and fetched the other two. I pulled out the costume and Jay enthused. She tried it on behind the screen. It was an almost fit but at least she and I could see as we looked at her reflection in the mirror that the design was good.

I pulled the cocktail dress from the rail in its plastic container. To my dismay I found the bodice unpicked. I burst into tears. One or two of the other girls came to look and then there were six or seven, still in the department who seemed to convene when they heard the commotion. The Prof appeared looking stern.

She looked at the dress. 'Does anyone know who did this?' she asked, but I knew no one would have known or if they did, they wouldn't say.

'Can you repair it Zandra?'

'If I have time. I may have to remake the bodice completely.'

'How long will that take.'

'Well most of the work is in the bodice, the stiffening, the boning. It was a perfect fit.'

'Tomorrow you start on that. Leave the wedding dress now, we will get some volunteers to sew pearls and crystals, that is simple enough, you must have the cocktail dress ready for the term end show, there are important people coming.

'Go home. Try not to think about it, but rest assured I want to get to the bottom of this.'

She took my dresses and their covers and hangers to her office.

I walked home with Jay. We stopped at the 'Pike and Lure' pub by the river.

'Come on, let's have a drink.' Jacquie said. 'You bag that table and I will get the drinks.'

I took the table that had the benefit of some privacy, sun, and shelter from the still cool wind.

She returned and we sat together, facing the sun. We said nothing. A young man appeared with a bottle of pinot grigio and two glasses. 'You aren't working tonight are you?' she asked.

'No two days off yet.'

"Let's get a little tipsy.'

She told me about her brothers, one older and one younger. There were plans for our stay.

'Have you spoken to Auntie yet?'

'Yes. I told her I would visit in the holidays; I have something important to tell her. She wanted to know what, but I said, it was too personal over the phone. She said, 'Very well dear.' That was all.

'Do you think she knows?'

'I don't know. Maybe she had discussed me with mum who I know had her suspicions. I mean I was not exactly a normal boy.'

We finished the bottle and walked home arm in arm. We cooked chilli for everyone, including Gemma's boyfriend. We drank while we cooked, giggling together in the kitchen. I felt better about things. The chilli was surprisingly good considering two drunks had cooked it. Gemma's boy was nice, Charlie, an athlete and doing a masters in physics.

Over the next week I managed to remake the bodice and reattach the skirt. It was no longer perfect and I still smarted from the attack on my work. For the first time as either boy or girl in fashion, I felt threatened.

"Bloody shame,' said Ainsley, sarcastically it seemed, and I wondered.

Chapter 15.

Our big show each year was the graduation show which would come next year for me, but the end of term shows still attracted store and manufacturing representatives looking for early talent, to sponsor and to sign up for employment after graduation, or to be interns during the vac.

It was normal for fashion designers to ask other students to model for them. In my case, I had designed the dresses and made them to fit me, so I would have to dress myself and go out on the catwalk. It seemed an impossible task, to do my makeup, dress and model, but when talking about it, Sue and Jacquie stepped up. Sue would be my dresser; Jacquie would do makeup, using her actor's equipment. Gemma and Charlie were going to be in the audience. I suggested that Jacquie should wear the wedding dress and after some persuasion she agreed. I had to let the bust out a bit, but I could manage that, I still had four days.

Jay practised some new makeup looks on my face, purple blusher, golden eye shadow, huge false lashes, smaller false lashes and lipsticks in blue, green and purple. She made a note of what she would do.

The day came at last. We had a non-dress rehearsal and went back at five for the real thing. I used a push up bra to give the impression of breasts. Sue was a good dresser and helped me into the little suit, fitted peplum jacket and skirt three inches above the knee, cunningly cut on the bias with an asymmetric flare. Prof doubted whether it could be done, but with clever use of webbing I pulled it off. The outfit was in pale bluebell, a really sweet colour. Jay did my daytime makeup and I wore large fake tortoiseshell specs. I looked like a secretary from a 1950s movie. My shoes were sprayed to match the suit.

Seventh out, and it proved lucky, it was well received. I did a more or less good impression of a model's strut and returned to the dressing room.

Next was the remade cocktail dress with black patent shoes, five inch heels the highest I had ever worn, bought out of the show budget and which would belong to me later. Dress on, as much bust as I could muster and both my friends did my evening make up, darkly framed eyes, brows highlighted, cheeks plumped with shadowing, cheeks highlighted to match the underskirt, false lashes. She caught my hair up, twisted it into a roll and fixed it with a pin. It was slightly Holly Golightly.

I strutted, making short steps, feeling like a dressage horse. I managed not to skate on a heel, the tulle underskirts swirling around my legs and when I pirouetted at the end of the platform, there was a burst of applause from an otherwise quiet crowd. I turned again and did a deep curtsy, hands and arms out prettily like a ballerina. Another burst of applause, longer this time I turned and made it back safely.

'Phew,' I said, 'that was nerve racking. They liked it.'

'I think they liked you just as much as the dress; there was a lot of goodwill there from other students too. Right, the wedding dress. I'm all made up, I just need to get it on.' Jacquie said.

Dear Jacquie struggled into the dress. It was quite tight on the bust even though I had let it out. She added a scarlet garter to her right thigh, white satin shoes. She struggled into the tightly boned bodice and hung on while I pulled and pulled on the stringing pulling her waist in impossibly small and as she did so the skirt belled out. The hem was asymmetric, deeper at the rear, below what was a built in bustle effect of extra net. The pearls and crystals glinted and shook as she moved and the garter just showed occasionally, tempting and seductive. Her hair was down, curled and fluffed with spray and brought over her right shoulder, kept in place by the tiara and a couple of combs. She caught sight of herself in the mirror and liked what she saw. Jay added some glitter dust after the hairspray, so her hair really glistened.

Prof sotto voce, 'Go they are waiting and this is the last.'

She progressed slowly, holding the fake bouquet, quickly thrust into her hand, making sure her steps were one in front of the other, creating a slight sway. The spot picked her up and the whole outfit came to life. The applause started tentatively and gradually escalated, and from the back where Gemma was with her boyfriend came 'Yo, yo yo.' It continued until Jay was finally behind the curtain.

Prof turned me around and kissed my cheek holding my hands. 'Come with me.' She commanded. She marched me out to take a bow, Jay on my other arm. Prof then asked for hush.

'May I present a true talent, Zandra Gregson, I am sure you will hear of her in the future. It has been a remarkable term for her, because she missed the first six weeks due to the death of both parents in a terrible crash, a change of gender and having one of her creations sabotaged just last week. She had to remake the cocktail dress, almost completely. I am very proud to have Zandra as my student.'

There was a stunned silence, followed by a ripple of applause that grew and grew as people took in the full meaning of her words. Prof and I embraced and then Jay and I kissed.

Afterwards in the crush, now in my ordinary clothes and clutching a glass of less than cold cheap fizz, I received many congratulations and a few business cards thrust into my hand, asking me to get in touch when I graduated in a year's time. I had hoped for sponsorship but at least I had interest.

Of course our show was just one of twenty or thirty around the UK so it was a very competitive market.

I saw the Prof talking to Ainsley. He was in tears. Last I saw two security men were escorting him from the room.

It looked as though the saboteur had been found. I had always had difficulty with Ainsley, one of those people that took an instant dislike and he had been like that with me, even worse since my transformation. He had seemed out of place, completely different to the other fashionistas, aggressively male, big built and unrefined. If he had gone, then I was relieved.

That I had been outed to the public was another matter. I wondered whether the Prof had even thought about it. Oh well, I thought, in this fashion milieu, it was hardly important. She must have assumed that I was truly out and when I thought about it, there was no way I could not be.

Team Zandra got together with Gemma and Charlie and we made for the Wall of China where Jay had booked a table.

We had the deluxe meal for five or six on a round table where we could spin the dishes around. We drank Tsingtao lager. We left just after midnight and went straight home.

I lay in in the morning. My mouth was dry, I was thirsty and a lingering sweet sour taste persisted. I used the bathroom and scrubbed my teeth, gums and tongue and rinsed my mouth for some time. I washed my hair under the shower, seeing the last of the sparkles run down the drain.

I dried my hair and dressed. I went down and found Gemma and Charlie already drinking coffee. I made tea and asked if they would like porridge as I was making. They declined. I sat eating my plateful, legs curled up in an armchair, when I heard the front door open and Jacqueline appeared with a bag of hot cross buns. She had a newspaper under her arm.

'Hi,' I said.

'Hi you all.' She replied in her Southern States drawl she so loved.

Having left the buns in the kitchen, she reappeared with the newspaper. She sat on the arm of my chair and ruffled my hair affectionately.

'You had better see this.' She handed me the local morning rag.

I looked at the headline. 'Triumph over Sabotage' a picture of me on the catwalk in the cocktail dress and a smaller one of Jay in the wedding dress, neither good photos, I think taken without flash as photos were banned. However, it was unmistakably me and there followed an article that gave my name as Zandra Gregson, female transgender designer. Oh god, I was truly outed then.

Gem asked to see.

'So! This is not the dark ages, people are much more accepting these days. What are you worrying about and flushing over?'

'Well Gemma, there are people out there who do not like transgendered people and frankly I just want to live my life as a female. I do not want to be placed in a different class of humanity. I hate labels. I don't understand why gay people like to be classified according to whom they love.

Jacquie put her arm across my shoulder and bent and kissed my head. 'I can understand that. Its like they would say about you Gemma, 'Gemma Anderson, former virgin of 16 Trafalgar Gardens, presently fucking Charlie Summers.'

Everyone fell about laughing. Sue, who had just come down and stood in the doorway, nearly collapsed having caught Jay's speech but not what had preceded it.

She caught up. 'Thing is, as far as I know, and I hasten to add, I have not been there, gay people do like to go to gay pubs and clubs, whereas transsexuals like our little Zandie, just want to merge silently into the female population on equal terms. I can understand that. Why does everyone have to be categorised according to sexuality and gender? I guess people think I am gay or something because I have yet to find a boy I am interested in.'

'What about a girl?' Jacquie said with a laugh.

'Mm, I do love girls, that is why I live here with you guys, but not for sex. I am not one for just having a boy for the sake of saying I have one. There has to be some spark for me to be interested. Anyway, I have never asked, but while we are on this track we have other bachelors here. Jacquie, who rocks your boat?'

'There was a boy, his name was Bill,' she sang, 'oh a few dates, but never the right one. I suppose one could keep one chained for sex, otherwise it can be a lot of grief for nothing. The right one and I think I will recognise him when we meet, like in South Pacific, 'Some enchanted evening, there will be a stranger, there will be a stranger, across a crowded room, and then I will know, I'll know even then, that somehow I'll see him, again and again.' She sang beautifully.

We all clapped. 'You are so talented,' Gemma said.

'Oh I know, and you think I am an airhead at times, but you will see my name up in lights one day. And we have one left to say who she fancies.'

She looked at me and I burst out laughing in confusion. 'I? I can't answer that.'

'It's Gino or Guiseppe.' Sue said.

'Most certainly not. I don't know. I am not yet equipped to make a decision, am I? And God knows how I will feel after being filled with hormones. At the moment I am pretty well sexless. I like being with girls, because that is whom I identify with and like. I love my life here with you all. Could I live with you all forever? That is another matter and for another time.'

Jay squeezed my hand. 'Let's all go to that pub if our designer will drive us. Beer and a burger.'

"I am OK with that, but Charlie is in the back with two of you. You can fight over him and who sits in the front. It may be a bit of a squeeze.'

'Oh I am in the front with my project.' Jay said.

So we set off and we had a good time eating pub food and drinking beer. I was not recognised so I thought, I had not been made famous or notorious. In any case, who is really bothered about a transsexual frock designer.

That night and the next five nights I was at the old Kettle. Gino and Guiseppe were very complimentary about the article in the paper but none of the customers seemed to recognise me. I was thankful for that.

Chapter 16.

Jacquie and I left for her home as soon as term ended. The drive took just an hour on a blustery and showery late March day. We listened to the radio and she sang along as I drove. She had an incredible voice, perfect pitch she told me. It was a delightful, intimate short journey.

When we left the main road, she gave directions down country lanes, warning me to beware of sharp bends and hidden entrances as though I was a complete novice. It was well meant. Eventually we turned through a grove of birch and oak and right again up a hedged drive. Suddenly before us was a huge Georgian house, red brick and stone mullions, three wide steps up to a porticoed doorway. I drew to a stop in the wide gravelled drive before the house.

'Well, here we are, home.'

'It looks terrific. We lived in a barn conversion, but this is something else. How many bedrooms?'

'Eight, not including the attics which were for the staff. We had more but some are now bathrooms. We only have one maid who lives in and Martha who comes from the village to clean.'

As we pulled bags from the boot, two young men came out of the front door.

'OK sis?'

The eldest grabbed her and kissed her cheek then she went to the second and kissed him.

'Zandra this hairy brute with the dreadful beard is Dom, Dominic and this is my younger brother, Gerard. My friend Zandra.'

'The fabulous Zandra. I have heard so much about you, third hand of course.' Dom said. Before I knew what he was doing, Dom had taken hold of me and kissed me on the lips.

'Hmm, well that was OK, tasted good,' he said.

I blushed. Gerard kissed me in the French manner. He grabbed my bag. 'Come on; don't mind Dom, he likes to shock. I'll show you your bedroom; it's next to Jay's. We live just across the corridor on the second floor.'

We crossed the black and white tiled floor to a handsome staircase, a metre and a half wide with carved banisters. It was wine red carpeted and possessed two landings to reach the first floor. It continued in like fashion to the second floor. We turned into a quite dark passageway with doors off. He opened one as we passed.

'That is Jay's, the next is your shared bathroom, then this is yours. You have morning sun, so I hope you are an early riser.' He placed my case on a case stand just inside. 'I'll leave you to sort yourself out. See you later.'

He left, closing the door.

I surveyed the room. It was old fashioned, old furniture, dark brown wood, and a small four-poster bed with white net drapes. A large sash window looked out on parkland.

I hung my clothes and put the rest in the chest of drawers. I entered the bathroom via the connecting door and found that Jay had also opened her door to the bathroom. I could see her changing in her room. I took in her very beautiful body clad in black lace underwear. I moved quickly away, embarrassed, not wishing to be thought a voyeur.

I set out my toiletries, leaving space for hers. As I was returning to my room she said, 'Don't be shy, you can come in.'

I did as bidden, shyly, diffidently, not knowing where to look. She seemed to have no such inhibitions, sitting in bra and panties, painting her toenails.

'I was tired of that red colour I just had to change it. It's funny how we can paint our finger nails, any colour, multi colours and yet it seems the convention to paint toe nails is red or at least pink.'

She was painting hers turquoise. She finished.

'Needs another coat. Come on, I'll do yours. Get those tights off.'

I did as bidden. It was strange. I had never been in this proximity to a girl in her underwear before but within minutes, as she attended to my toes, I felt quite at home.

'Nice feet, no bunions,' she said. 'We both need another coat and a topcoat. We will be toenail twins.' She laughed at her own silliness.

'How do you feel, sitting here with a nearly nude woman? Does it disturb you?'

'No, well yes slightly. It is a first. I mean I have no sisters, not even a brother.'

'Are you shy about people seeing your body?'

'I am, but only I think, because it is the wrong body. I mean if I didn't have a penis and I had breasts, then I think I would have no inhibitions at all.'

'What none, say my brothers walked in and you had a female body. What then?'

'If I was dressed like you in bra and pants, no, I don't think I would be shy. Maybe apprehensive.'

'Oh that is interesting. Apprehensive! Why, because they might jump on your bones or because you think they might not like what they see?'

'I suppose both. I may be a boy physically, but mentally I am not. I do not understand boys. I don't relate to them at all. I don't trust them.'

'Well you are wise not to trust them, naughty little blighters. Why don't you take your things off like me?'

'Because I hate my body as it now is, it is too boy.'

'But I have seen it before. In your room getting you ready for the café and the fashion show, a number of different occasions.'

'Yes but here, now, why?'

'Because if you were an ordinary girl, this might be how we would be.' She smiled and laid a hand on my arm. Those lovely blue eyes and long lashes, her exquisite lips.

'I wish I had your body and looks. I would be so happy.'

'Come, don't be shy.' She proceeded to remove my top and blouse. She unzipped my skirt.

'Stand up and step out of your skirt. Sit on the bed with me.'

'There. See. The ceiling has not fallen in on us, on you. I don't want you to be shy with me at all. Promise you won't be. Swear. I am your sister.'

'I swear. I'll try.'

'You feel OK?'

'Yes, just I can manage the breast thing, I mean not having any, but what is between my legs, that is a severe embarrassment to me, a horror.'

'Ah my poor baby. Are you OK? You can dress again if you want.' I shook my head.

'No it is OK, until we finish our toes at least.'

'Look at my enormous bed, a six foot four-poster, a present from Daddy on my fourteenth birthday. Mum curses it because the washing machine can only do one sheet or duvet-cover at a time. Why don't you sleep in here with me? I would love you too.'

'Gosh you are a funny girl. Do you really want me to?'

'Of course. It will be fun.'

'OK, I will.'

'I think our toes are dry now. Shall we get dressed, have some lunch and see what the boys are up to. Don't mind Dom, he has always been outrageous. He likes to embarrass, but he is the kindest person really. Do you want to freshen your makeup, or are you OK. You look OK, perhaps a little lippy.'

We got ourselves together. On the way down she showed me the other rooms, her parents room, was huge, the guest rooms ornate.

We explored the ground floor, a large drawing room, a dining room, a breakfast room and morning room, a study and a sitting room, the domain of father and her mother respectively.

We went to the kitchen and found the boys munching toast.

'We have been waiting for you girls to make some lunch, thought you would have been down long ago.' Dom said.

'Boys, you have to learn, girls have given up waiting on men. We are all equal now; it is the age of the new man. You may not have babies, but when you wed and produce them, you will be expected to mind them, change them, walk the vacuum around the house and feed the washing machine and tumble dryer. No good making out you don't understand the domestic machines. If you can manage to use a computer, you can do all these chores. Women have seen through men at last.'

'Dear Sis, we thought better of you. Have you become a suffragette? Is this your malign influence Zandra?'

'No, not at all.'

'Oh no boys, it is modern life. You had better get used to it.'

'What are you guys having for lunch,' Gerard asked.

'Mm some soup I think. Daddy says we are eating out tonight, so we only want a little snack and it seems, you boys have had your lunch. Is soup OK for you Zandie?'

'Fine, can I help?'

'You watch the soup and I will make the toast and put the kettle on for a drink. Tea or coffee?'

'Coffee please.' Dom said.

'I wasn't speaking to you, lazy bones. What did they teach at Eton? Zandie, what would you like?'

'I think tea please.'

'I guess Gerry, we have lost our domestic slave. Make us a coffee.'

'I'll make me one. You are on your own Dom.'

'Have all my slaves lost their minds? Zandie, precious girl, can you make coffee?'

'Actually no. I am not fond of it, so I make it very badly. Why can't you?'

'I don't understand that machine.'

'Then dear little Dominic, I suggest you read the manual. I know boys find that demeaning but it does help.'

'Well done Zandie. You are learning.'

We held out.

Chapter 17.

After lunch she showed me round the estate. First we visited the stables, and then she took a quad bike and drove us around. The estate was large, the land let to a neighbouring farmer, but it was laid out so that the horses could be used safely around it, with wide headlands to canter down.

When we returned the boys were behaving themselves, no longer trying to make slaves of us or pretending helplessness. They chatted about Uni and asked us about our courses. I wondered what to tell them as I did not know whether they too were aware of my past or my present status.

Luckily Jay could answer for me and give a lead. They were apparently oblivious of my past I thought. They were quite interested in my fashion exploits and I was surprised when Jay fetched her phone and showed shots of me. She had given her phone to Charlie and he had snapped away.

'Hey they are brilliant. Clever girl. You look absolutely smashing there, well now too, but with that makeup, beautiful. Oh and sis too, in a wedding dress.'

'That was thanks to your talented sister, she did the makeup and Sue another housemate was my dresser. Jacqueline made a super bride didn't she.'

'She did, does.

'Yes she helped me with the changes, like in the theatre and I thought she would make a better bride than me.'

'And do you get a prize for best or something?'

'If you are lucky someone gets in touch with an offer to employ you, one of the big fashion houses or a manufacturer.'

'You seem very serious.'

'About what?'

'Just everything.'

'She is quite shy, but we giggle a lot when we are together, Don't we Zand?'

I nodded. "You have a very funny, zany sister. And she is clever too. What are you boys doing?'

'I'm doing law, Gerry will tell you what he does. I don't understand it.'

'Electric and Electronic engineering. It is not that complicated, Dom thinks it is because he is not at all a scientist. I find the law far more of a tangled web. Didn't someone say, 'the law is an ass'?'

'Mr Bumble in Oliver Twist for one,' I said. 'He said it because the judge said that the law held the husband responsible for the wife's behaviour.'

'Then Mr Bumble was correct.'

"You will find that does not pertain today,' Dom said, putting his book down. 'Since women became emancipated and have equal rights, it no longer applies. At one time a wife was considered a chattel and all her assets became the husbands on marriage, but so did the debts too.'

'There see, Dom is not a complete airhead, just lazy.' Jay said. 'I think mummy has arrived. Come and meet her.' She took me by the hand and we left the room. Her mother had just pushed her way in the front door and we met in the hall.

'Mummy, this is Zandra.'

'I am so pleased you could come and redress the male female balance. I have heard all about you, so it is nice to meet at last. My word, you are pretty. Please call me Samantha.'

'Mummy, she is not out, if you understand. I have not told the boys.'

'Oh I see. That is fine, I'm not sure whether they know or not. Anyway, we are eating out tonight, seven-thirty at the Bear and Staff. If father does not get home in time he will meet us there. It is not dressy, so don't fret Zandra, that you haven't a posh frock.'

'Oh good. Well I have some reasonably smart clothes.'

'Zandra is an accomplished waitress mummy as well as a celebrated dress designer.'

'Really, are you Zandra. How do you find the time?'

'I just have to. The good thing about being a fashionista is that most of what counts is done in design and the cutting room, so when not actually in college I can devote myself to something else. Waitressing pays the rent and keeps me in clothes.'

'Come into the kitchen and have a cup of tea with me girls. I am exhausted. These committees go round and round without ever making a sensible decision it seems.'

We followed her into the kitchen and sat drinking tea. As she unwound, she became friendlier and less distant. She rose and shut the kitchen door.

'So do you have many difficulties Zandra?'

I told her about my life. I told her how Jay had made me up in the loo to get the waitress job and how she took me to have my ears pierced and the other support she had given me.

"I owe her a lot, I really do. From the day we met, she saw into my soul and brought out my inner self. I would have got there but it would have taken me much longer. Now I have to face up to telling my family, well my Aunt, mum's sister.'

'What a shame you have to go all through this. I'm glad it was my clever daughter enabled you. As you have discovered she is the sweetest girl.

'Now I need to freshen up. I am going to shower and change into something less formal and we'll leave here at seven. I think we can all cram into my car unless your father comes home, then we will use two. Whatever, we shall have two cars to return in. I'll see you downstairs at seven.'

We went up to shower and change too.

I put on one of the two dresses I possessed, a dark blue shirtwaister with long sleeves and turn back cuffs. I looked for jewellery to pretty it up but realised I really had nothing that was worthy.

I did my hair and was starting on my makeup when Jay walked in.

'That colour really suits,' she said, 'nice dress. Where did you get that.'

'JL sale, with my second week's money. It was a bit of a steal I think at fifty pounds.'

'I like it. But it needs something, something really bright. Let me do your makeup. Can I? I want to make you really sultry and mysterious.'

'Can blondes be sultry and mysterious?'

'Deffo. And you my dear sister will be.'

She moisturised and mixed a tiny amount of moisturiser with foundation and worked that over my skin with her fingers. She kept surveying my face as she would a canvass. She defined my brows, combing them after pencilling, lined my eyes with a tiny pointed brush and used charcoal and silver eye shadow, blending it with the very tip of her small finger. She added two blushers, a very dark one below a lighter rose one, giving the effect of sunken cheeks. She applied four coats of mascara, each coat quite light but the effect was separate lashes impressively long. She added a quite dark red lipstick. Only then was I allowed to see her finished painting.

'Wow! I think in this light I'm even quite beautiful.'

'Don't you know? You are beautiful. Without makeup, you are still pretty. I have merely added character. So you are pleased with what I have done?'

'Yes, my dear Jacquie. I love you. Whatever happens in life after Uni, when you are a famous star in California or in lights on Broadway or the West End, I will always remember you with love and unending gratitude for the love and generosity you have shown a poor misfit.'

She put her arms around me, her cheek against mine. 'I love you too, from the minute you arrived at our house, like a frightened rabbit that didn't want me to help. Now, I think I have the very things to brighten you up.'

She departed and within a minute returned with a jewellery box, she opened it to reveal a pearl bracelet, necklace and a silver and pearl broach in the form of a tree branch. She soon adorned me. I loved it when she lavished attention, dressing me, doing my hair or makeup.

'There, you shall go to dinner. You look absolutely fab. My brothers will be smitten. Keep them at arms length if you want to preserve your privacy.'

'I don't know. I might think about being out and proud, I mean to friends and of course if I ever become famous. If transsexuals are ever to get over the prejudice and stigma, then we have to be out and show that we are not weird and not monsters.'

'Think about it first. Certainly not tonight. Daddy knows and mummy, the boys don't, not from me anyway. I will find out whether they do and we go from there. I think you are right, and if there were to be something in the media, then I would think you need to be honest, perhaps with friends too, for the sake of other trans people, but for you personally, I am not sure.'

'OK. I will keep mum for the moment.'

'Don't see why you should have to sacrifice your privacy for the sake of 'the cause', transsexuals acceptance by the World at large.'

'Perhaps it is up to us all to be 'out' and proud. That is how gays got acceptance.'

'Well maybe, when you are post op and successful, but not now.'

We collected in the hall at seven. The boys had scrubbed up quite well, still in jeans but with proper shoes, nice shirts and leather bombers. Their mother wore a trouser suit in off white, very elegant, with three-inch heels. Jay had what looked like a silk dress in a dark flower pattern and five inch patent stilettos. My four inch heels looked OK, but not near as good as her Christian Louboutins. She still looked like a bird to me. She caught me appraising her and looked back from the side of her eyes and stuck her tongue out. I giggled.

'You look divine,' I said.

'And you are delectable.'

'You are both gorgeous.' Gerry said.

Dom winked at me. He took my hand. 'We are in the back. Do you mind being in the middle, only we have such long legs?'

'Right off we go,' Samantha said picking up her bag and taking her keys. 'Dom lock up please.'

He set the alarm, slipped the catch and tested the door as we piled into the Mercedes. I was going to sit in the middle but was called to sit in the front passenger seat. 'Take no notice of my boys, any chance to feel a female thigh. They will have to make do with their sister. We will have more room on the way home, Daddy is meeting us there.'

We drove through quiet roads, crossed the A11 and carried on into Cambridge. Samantha was a good driver, a positive one and gave confidence. I was warm and cosy. I loved my life and it was all thanks to Jay.

Samantha parked right by the door and we were soon crowding through it, out of the cold night air and into the low light of the warm restaurant.

We were quickly shown to our table. The boys went to the bar to buy drinks, a white wine spritzer for Samantha, two G and Ts for Jay and me and they were having real ale, something called Ram's Head that was apparently their favourite.

Five minutes later their father Ralph arrived. He looked tired but he immediately began to tease his children and I could see from where the boys got their naughtiness. He kissed Sam and Jay, then me. I was quite surprised, but it was lovely to be included.

Menus were provided but there was so much chatter in the family, catching up with each other as well as a few questions for me, that we were not decided when the waiter came. He would come a little later he said and we got down to studying the carte and table d'hote.

I decided on Prawn Normande to start followed by magret à la d'Artagnan, duck my favourite.

'Ah we have a connoisseur as well as a beautiful young dress designer,' Ralph said. 'I think I might follow suit.'

Eventually we all gave our orders.

'Zandra is a waitress,' Samantha said, 'so no doubt she will be watching with a professional eye.'

'I am a good waitress by Italian standards, so my employers have told me. I love it. We have great fun and I do like serving people, doing it well. I have no other income.'

'So how much does that pay?' Dom asked.

'Don't be rude,' Samantha said.

'I don't mind saying. My pay is £10 per hour for five evenings a week, six till eleven. I go at six and eat there, so that is a meal I have free. Then we get our own tips, Guiseppe extracts them from the payment and pays us individually. He says that way there is no argument and the better one performs the higher the tips. I clear between £50 and £100 in tips each week, sometimes more if I have particularly generous customers.'

'That's good money.' Gerard said. 'Can you study as well?'

'In normal hours. There is not a lot of home study in fashion, I mean there is background, history, technical things like the way materials are constructed and of course, the great fashion movements, the New Look and Mary Quant, even Norman Hartnell, and of course Chanel and Dior and the influencers of fashion over the last century. One has to know all those things, but that is only background reading. Most of it is hands on, design, creative design and using a computer these days to convert your initial sketch into a production item. Then there is cutting and sewing, presentation skills, marketing and finance.'

'Oh, so a lot more than just making a pretty frock.'

'I should think so.'

'Zandra is very talented.' Jay said proudly with affection.

'Were you really a boy?' Gerard asked.

If that question had been asked of me a month ago, I would have wanted to fall through a trap door into a dark cellar. I think this time I did not even blush.

'Hush Gerard,' Samantha said.

'Reasonable question. I don't understand how a woman this beautiful could have been a proper man. It is impossible, I mean….' He subsided into confusion.

'So we all know. I was debating with Jacquie about telling you tonight. She said no, why should I? I thought I should actually tell everyone, so that the world's opinion of transsexuals is not so negative. To answer your question, yes I was a boy, not a very good one, not a boy's boy. And I was miserable. So, well I may as well tell you of my past. I always thought, identified with being a girl, from earliest memories, I hated myself because my body was not as it should be, I could not wear the clothes I wanted to or do what I felt I should. Father was very cross if I was at all girlie. I self-harmed, common among pre-transition transsexuals, as is suicide, up to fifty per cent among those who for one reason or another cannot change. Oh dear, it is too long a speech.'

'No it is fascinating. Now having met you, I want to know more. To me, happy in my man skin, I find it hard to understand. Why, why were you not happy to be a boy.'

'Because of the way my brain is wired. They used to think it was nurture. Now they believe it has nothing to do with that, it is in the brain, the psyche. Just as a woman is programmed to have children, to accept the dangers and pain of childbirth, we are programmed with brains the opposite of our natal sex.'

The waiter arrived with the starters. Wine was poured and our first glasses were removed. We ate busily, the boys at high speed as though they had been starved for a week.

Samantha steered the conversation away from me, to what the arrangements were for the summer vacation. Gerry tried to bring it back to me.

'No more Gerry, not here. At home if Zandra doesn't mind and find you intrusive but this is too public. There are other guests here now.'

Dom said he was off to Chile, climbing in the summer. Gerard was going to China with a group of students, looking at the enormous electronics factories.

Jay said she was not going anywhere, making no plans in case she was offered a part. I said I had nowhere to go except to my aunt, that I might stay in our house for most of it and carry on working for Guiseppe and Gino.

'Well I think you should come to us. I know Jacquie would love to have you here.'

'Of course I would. She has to tell her family yet though. We are going to see her aunt on Tuesday.'

'Well it does not have to be that much of a big deal? I mean, really. It is not the end of the world is it?'

'Some people seem to think so. Someone sabotaged one of my dresses, so not everyone is happy with me. Can we talk about someone else please, for instance, you boys, have you girl friends?'

They spun the usual stuff about playing the field and not wanting a serious relationship.

'So boys, I take it you are both still virgins?' I said provocatively.

Samantha choked on her wine. 'Well boys,' she said, 'I would like an answer to that question. Well-done Zandra. Turned the tables. So come on you two.'

Dom looked at me as though he was seeing someone afresh. Gerry had turned red. Jacquie burst out laughing.

'OK sis, if it so funny, then why not tell us whether you have or haven't.'

'A lady's prerogative to keep her secrets my brothers. One thing I can tell you is that my friend here will not play your silly games. She will give as good as she gets.'

'And we do not kiss and tell,' Dom retorted.

'Mmm, Dom, they say there are two reasons to grow a beard, one is to attract girls that other is to hide behind it. Lot's of gay men for example have beards.'

'You have a sharp tongue Miss Zandra. If you were a Shakespeare character, I see you as Kate in Taming the Shrew.'

'And Hamlet said when he was handed a skull, 'Alas, poor Yorick', he mused on the skull - 'why may not that be the skull of a lawyer?' Jay quoted.

'Ouch, these girls are sharp! They look like roses and they have prickles to boot.' Dom said.

'That could be Shakespeare, but I don't think it is.' Jay said.

'Do what thou dar'st; I'll beard thee to thy face.' I said.

'Wow! Who said that?'

'If I remember rightly, the Bishop of Winchester in Henry six, but I think I heard it in the TV play, the Red and the White.'

'There is nothing either good or bad, but thinking makes it so.' Gerry quoted, 'That is Hamlet and that is how I feel. And dear girls, neither Dom nor I drive on the other side of the road. We just have not met such charming ladies as yourselves to waste our time and money on.'

'Well I must say. An expensive education seems to have paid off.' Samantha said.

'I went to a Comp.' I said.

'Then you must have been an exceptional student.' Ralph said. 'You are certainly a match for these boys.'

'She's a bright girl. I commend my dear sister on her choice of friend.' Dom said.

I blushed.

After that the meal was very informal, witty and relaxed. Dom kept glancing at me across the table. I raised an eyebrow towards him and he grinned.

We all had sweets, I had crème brûlée, then it was on to the coffee and the boys had liqueurs.

We were home just after midnight, feeling a little squiffy.

I took off my makeup and showered. I put on my PJs and went through the communicating doors. Jay was in bed already. She patted the bed and I slid in. She put the light off. We chattered for a bit.

'First time you have slept with a girl and you don't want to make love to her. You really are a girl aren't you my sweet darling Zandie. Thank you for being my friend.'

'Thank you, for everything. Without you, I might not be here.' I kissed her on the lips and turned my back. She snuggled in tight and put her arm across my waist, her hand across my stomach. It was delightful, the most contact I'd had with a human in the last sixteen years.

Chapter 18.

It was delicious to wake up with my best friend, even more delectable that she always treated me as female.

I lay thinking about my life and the turn it had taken since knowing Jay. I turned and watched her, lying absolutely motionless, her sweet face in repose just as pretty, as bird like as when she was awake. Her eyelids flickered and her eyes opened momentarily.

'Hi', I said. 'Did you sleep well?'

'Mmm. Very well. It was nice having you here but I don't remember anything.'

'I have never slept with anyone else, no sisters or brothers. I don't think I ever had a sleep over either.'

'We sometimes bunked up at Cheltenham, weren't supposed to but if we were cold or upset, we would. It is so comforting.'

'Are there any plans for today?'

'Mmm not sure. Have you anything you want to do?

"It's Sunday. Do you all go to church or anything?'

'You must be kidding. We usually relax; mum cooks a roast in the afternoon. We could ride this morning; actually I would like to, I haven't ridden for weeks. Would you mind if we did that?'

'I don't ride.'

'Well perhaps this is your opportunity. I'll look after you. I have jodhpurs that will fit and spare boots, jacket and helmet. I'd like to se you in riding gear.'

'So would I.'

'Well then, shower and I will sort some clothes for you. Then breakfast or probably brunch. The boys may have plans that include us too.'

I showered and was in undies by the time Jay gave me clothes to wear. Before I dressed, she sat me down and plaited my hair. I almost purred. While she showered I dressed and did my face. I looked at the horsewoman in the mirror and chuckled. I really liked what I saw. I felt more confident over my appearance every day. I felt pain in my chest. It was quite tender.

Jay came through fully dressed, her hair caught in a bun. She looked so brilliant.

'My chest is tender. I can't remember bumping in to anything.'

'Why, ma po honey chile, that's your breasts growin'.' she said.

'Oh crikey. I suppose it is. This is brilliant. This must be the best pain ever. Do girls have this pain in puberty?'

'Of course. The hormones must work on your body the same as my natural ones did. They will be painful for quite a long time.'

'Well I shan't mind that. It's just so great that they are developing.'

'Not all girls have breast development. It varies a lot. Girls with anorexia get hardly anything. I'm so pleased for you. Keep on taking the hormones, don't miss, eat properly, and I'm sure you will produce a good pair of chest puppies.'

We giggled together like teenagers.

Downstairs we found that bacon and egg butties were on offer. The boys were not up yet. We drank tea and ate a butty and went to the stables.

Jacquie groomed both horses, warning me to stay out of the way in case they kicked or bit. She tacked up, explaining as she did so, but I could not take it all in.

She lead out what was to be my mount, a mare that she assured me was quiet and well behaved, an easy ride.

I used the mounting block under instruction and was soon sitting in the saddle with Jay adjusting the stirrups. I felt high up and I realised how a mounted police officer can see so much more than one on foot and what an advantage they have in a crowd.

Jay mounted easily, her horse turning skittishly, but she made it look easy whereas I was sure to have been flung to the ground.

I had thought that riding was a matter of sitting on a horse, pulling on the reins and giving the occasional kick. I found that it was constant hard work, at least for a novice, and Jay seemed to keep up a constant stream of instruction and criticism. In fact she laughed, which I thought rather cruel, when I complained that my bum hurt from bouncing up and down. Then I noted and she told me, that one moved with the horse, at all times, and in the trot, instead of bouncing with each movement of the horse's leg, one bounced rhythmically, rising in the saddle. Even then one had to have timing and I failed miserably. We walked again. I was glad to do that, adopting the seat, so Jay told me, of a tired old cowboy.

Whereas she looked smart and in control, I looked like and felt like a sack of potatoes in a pickup truck driven over a ploughed field.

I was glad when she decided to return. The glamour of riding, the becoming jodhpurs, boots and hacking jackets I decided, were something to be worn but not ridden in by me. On the ground, crop in hand I looked the business, on top of a horse I was horse's doodahs.

The good thing was that Jay did not hold my ineptitude against me, and while she had laughed, it was in a kindly fashion.

Safely back in the stables, we took off saddles and bridles and groomed the horses again, this time allowing me to do my mount, called Sarah, which I happened to know, is Hebrew for Princess. We then fed and watered them. Apparently a girl came to muck out each evening in return for exercising the horses.

We entered the house by the back door, taking our boots off in the utility room. We had to clean them too. Anyway that occupied the morning, but my legs were tired and a little chafed. Jacquie had made it all look so graceful and natural, I was disappointed in myself and said so.

'Don't be, I have been riding since three years old, so it is second nature, like driving a car to you. Perhaps if we do it again, we will only do an hour and I think, in the school, the yard at the back and I will try to teach you. Or if you would rather not, we won't bother.'

'Whether I do or not, you should ride Jay, you love it and should do it. I can easily amuse myself for a couple of hours.'

'Whatever! Let us see what the boys are up to.'

We found them in the drawing room reading, apparently for their courses.

'We thought you might like to go out,' Jay said. How about we go to Southwold and sit in a pub. Then we can go to Snape and browse the antiques.'

'Whose driving if we are drinking?' Dom, asked.

'I will,' I said, 'as long as you don't drink too much and are not sick in my car.'

'We don't do that,' Gerry said.

'Just thought I would check.'

So I drove and we found a pub, not actually in Southwold but with good beers, found in their CAMRA directory, by a village pond. We found an empty sun lounge with deep, soft leather furniture. The sun streamed through the window and belied the bitter wind that blew from the North Sea.

'So now Zandie, what is it like being you. Are you having an exciting life?'

'I am now. Since I emerged from my male cocoon, thanks to your dear sister. Why now I am out with you aren't I? What more could a girl dream of.'

'A ready wit. Be careful or one day you may cut yourself with your tongue. But I am genuinely interested. It is a something we often hear about these days and people may be surprised, doubtful, sneering or understanding, well to a point, but no one knows how you think, feel.'

'I have all the hang-ups and worries of a girl my age, plus I have the added anxieties of whether I look female, whether people can see the boy behind the mask, whether I am acting like a female or whether my birth sex is showing. And behind that too, is the knowledge that medicine cannot undo completely what nature has done.'

'But I don't understand why you are doing this? What the driver is? Is it to be attractive to men?'

'If it was just that, I would be gay wouldn't I? I will try to explain fully. I don't know whether you in your short lives have hankered after anything, a toy, a car, a girl, a visit somewhere? I mean heart-achingly hankered as though it was the only thing that mattered?'

'Well perhaps, momentarily, like for a week, I really wanted an expensive skateboard. It seemed the only thing in my life that mattered, but it went away. After a few days, I was interested in something else.'

'Well with a woman, programmed to reproduce, failure to do so can be devastating, as you may realise, wanting a baby, the maternal instinct denied. You, as men, are programmed to fertilise as many women as possible, but society dictates monogamy. So to bring it down to the male level, if you were told you could never have sex in all your life, that to do so could be fatal, you would probably feel dysphoria. The meaning of dysphoria in case you do not know is melancholy, depression, anxiety and hundreds of other words for extreme mental anguish.

'All my instincts tell me to look, act, speak, have the body of, the sexual functions of a woman. I identify with Jacquie, not you. The deprivation of being able to express myself as a female, is like a sentence of death to my inner soul. I felt as though I was moving in a monochrome world Dom, now I feel I have entered Disneyland, the World is suddenly painted with colour, the birds sing, the raindrops on leaves are sparkling crystals, bunnies will pop out of burrows and wave. My grey hopeless world has become one of hope where I can be fulfilled. I know it must be very difficult to understand.'

'So it is not about us, about men, at all?'

'Hardly at all. Relationships with men may or may not be a part of the package. Some transsexuals, that's people who have transitioned, changed their gender, may still fancy people opposite to their natal sex, that is someone born a boy and becomes a girl, may still fancy girls.'

'I think I am getting it. So who do you fancy?'

'I'm waiting to see. I think probably, no I will not say. I am taking hormones and I may change. I know I love my girlfriends, but that is not sexual. I have not met many men. I was bullied by boys in my school, maybe that is why as yet, I have not learned to trust them.'

'It's all very complicated isn't it. I think I get it now. So can I ask one last question?'

'Ask but I don't know that I will answer it.'

'When you wake in the morning, what is your first thought?'

'That is a good question, the lawyer's mind working. Before Jacquie got to work on me, it was like, another day I had to drag my body through, as though my spirit had this awful burden on it's shoulders, like a bird weighed down with a rock and cannot fly. Now, in my new life, I am like a fledgling signet, knowing I will grow to be a beautiful swan one day and soar into the blue sky.'

'Yes but do you have one particular thought when you awake?'

'Does anyone. Do you? I suppose at the moment, when my life is all new and rose tinted, I'm thinking, I'm a girl, oh God at last I am a girl.'

'So is that what you thought this morning?'

'No, well yes, partly. I woke up with Jay this morning, we shared her bed because we were a bit cold last night. And I lay there thinking, how lucky I had been to meet her and, how beautiful she was.'

Jay was staring at me. I thought I had offended.

'It wasn't quite like that,' she said, 'I suggested that we share my bed and it was really comforting to have her there.'

Dom completely ignored this and returned to transsexualism.

'We did cover some of this in a lecture. There are still legal hoops aren't there? To be completely, lawfully female, you need a Gender Recognition Certificate, that allows change of birth certificate, access to female pension, change of all official records, but you can just live as female, change driving licence, passport, medical card et cetera.'

'To obtain a GRC, one has to have medical evidence of change like the very least is orchiectomy. You will have to look that up.'

Dom spoke to his phone and received the answer. 'Ouch,' he said. 'You are a brave girl.'

'I used not to be. I think I owe my life to Jacquie who divined my inner self and gave me the strength to become as I am. But it is not brave for me, it is having an ugly growth removed.'

Gerry looked up from his book that he had been pretending to read. 'Are you in love with sis?'

'I love her, yes, but not well, sexually, but as someone who cares for me and I care for her. Like if there were a fire in our house, I would not leave without her, without knowing she was safe.'

Jacquie stirred from her place deep within her corner of the soft leather couch we shared and bumped over to sit against me. 'It is mutual,' she said taking my hand and caressing it.

We made our way to the seaside and parked in a layby. We walked for half an hour, arm in arm, laughing and joking. Gerrard was a serious boy, Dom like his father, witty, quick and quite funny.

We returned in time to help with dinner. Roast lamb and it was delicious. Normal British food cooked well is as flavoursome and exciting as any ponced up haute cuisine, picture on a plate. Roast meet, roast potatoes, Yorkshire puddings, nicely cooked greens, yummy.

Chapter 19.

Tuesday dawned, a cold grey sky I could see through a chink in the curtains. I still shared her bed. I almost always woke first but today, I turned to find her watching me, propped on one elbow.

'Hello darling,' she said, 'so how are you today Zandie? Are you ready for auntie and uncle?'

'Yes I think so. I will know more when I am half an hour from their house. At the moment there is just slight apprehension. I hope she will be accepting, she is mum's sister, my closest relative, I mean there is my father's brother, but I am not even going to bother. I may send a letter.'

'I have been lying here thinking about you. You want to be a girl. Do you know anything about a girl's anatomy?'

'Only from things like Wiki and other internet sites.'

'So this orchiectomy is that what you plan to have? I have looked that up and it is surgical castration. That leaves you with a penis. Is that what you plan?'

'I don't think so. I want the whole thing, all a girl's working parts as far as possible.'

She blushed. She said hesitantly, 'Would you like to see what that means?'

'What, you mean….? If it is not too much.'

'You have to see before you can make that decision. I have read up what they will do to you. You will have a urethral opening rather than a penis, a vagina, a clitoris and labia minor and major, and a mound of Venus. You may or may not have sexual satisfaction in varying degrees. You can examine me intimately if you wish.'

I blushed, my face burned and I bit my lip. 'No, not if you regret it later. I could not bare losing you because you had regrets afterwards.'

'Don't be silly. It's nothing to what you will experience. Go and open the curtains, then come back and see what female anatomy looks like.'

I drew the curtains and light flooded in. I was pleased to see patches of blue developing in the grey sky.

I retuned to the bed. She now lay uncovered, her legs spread. I was almost overcome, not by passion but by pure love for this girl who gave me so much.

'Where to begin.' I said.

'The outside and work from top to bottom.'

She described the working parts as we went, parting herself and feeling herself, taking my finger and placing it as she described labia, clit and vagina. Her mound. I looked into her eyes and saw something going on in her head, but could not decide whether it was fear or amusement.

'You are lovely. I wish I could be you or born like that.'

'Now you know. Is that what you want?'

'Yes, oh yes, I cannot rid myself of my penis soon enough.'

'OK. Good, as long as you are sure and you understand what you get, what you do not get and what you have to do for the rest of your life, like keeping yourself clean inside and dilation.'

'You must have done a lot of reading. Why do you do all this for me, including this last gift, an intimate examination.'

'Because Zandie I love you. I feel I have made you, almost like giving birth. If you have ever raised a kitten or a puppy, you have this almost maternal love. I love you with that sort of intensity. I hope you understand?'

'I am very lucky to have landed with such friends, and especially, really especially, you. Yes. It was a good day when I met you. Embarrassing. I thought you saw me put my girlie stuff in the wardrobe that day and pretended even to myself, that you had not. Was it just that?'

'That allowed me to see into the inner you? No, all I saw was the adjustable shoulder string of a chemise, but that triggered me to really analyse the stranger that had entered our household. The way you moved, the way of speaking, convinced me that something was going on, that you were female rather than male. I decided to provoke you, first by playing with your hair, then make up and the whole kit. Bam! Converted. I have no regrets; I have not perverted you as Gem thought at first. Rather I asserted the true inner you. And here we are.'

'I can hardly believe I have come so far in such a short time. It is just ten weeks since we first met.'

'And in three hours we are due to meet Auntie and Uncle.'

'Oh yes, I think Auntie will be fine. Men think differently.'

It was only a thirty-mile drive to my Aunts and we left in good time. I had done my own makeup, not too over the top, and examined by my mentor, I passed.

As I drew nearer my Aunt's house, my anxiety increased. Jay had not allowed any compromise in my dress or anything else. "You have the right, to present as you wish to be, not watered down to be palatable to your uncle and aunt. The idea that you should turn up in jeans and a T, is just nonsense. You want to be a girl and will be, so you have to do what pleases you.'

I knew she was right and I wanted to look as perfect as possible. I felt there was actually more chance of acceptance if I looked convincing than if I was half hearted. I wore a nice frock, figure hugging, heels, bangles and my one girlie watch.

I pulled into the drive and Aunt was at the door before I had applied the handbrake. Jay was out quickly, and dragging her handbag, went straight to my Aunt, hand out to shake. I switched off and climbed out with my bag over my shoulder and walked around the car.

Aunt released herself from Jay and came towards me.

'Alex dear,' she said and gave me a kiss. 'Come in, we'll go into the kitchen where it is warm before seeing your uncle.'

'Hello Aunt. I am sorry if I am a shock.'

'Shush. Come on, in the warm.' She led the way into her kitchen where the Aga was always hot.

'Now coffee, tea, wine or G and T?'

I looked at Jay and we more or less said together, 'Coffee would be lovely.'

'Aunt, this is Jacqueline, she has helped me transition.'

'Oh that is so nice of you Jacqueline. If anyone was in need of a friend, it was Alex.'

She pushed the switch on the coffee machine and looked at it doubtfully. 'I hope I have done that right.'

'So what have you to tell me dear?'

'I am changing gender auntie, as you see.'

'Yes dear, my sister, your mother always thought you might. Anyway, you look very nice. So are you Alex or some fancy name?'

I could see Jay smothering a guffaw. 'They, my housemates, call me Zandra or Zandie or even Zand. I am using Zandra for my new identity.'

'Like Rhodes dear, yes rather apt. Well good, so what else has happened?'

I told her about the show and my work as a waitress.

'Lovely dear. So it has all worked out right. Just think; three months ago you were suicidal now look at you. Of course I knew all about your cross-dressing. I found your girlie clothes hidden under your undies. I said to your uncle, Mandy was right, that boy will not make a man.'

'So does Uncle know?'

'Oh I told him, but whether he knows, is another thing. You will find with men, that they say yes dear, when you tell them something, but it has blown straight into their brains and is lost somewhere in the space they keep for social graces.'

'Well I don't want to be a shock.'

'He will not even register the difference dear. Now it is salmon for lunch, I hope that is OK with you both?'

'Yes, we both eat salmon.'

'What do you study Jacqueline.'

'I'm a drama student.'

'Oh, will I have seen you in anything yet?'

'I made an advert that has been on national TV and a bit in a film. So I am getting there I hope.'

'And you are looking after er, Zandra?'

'She is Aunty I owe her so much. She has been brilliant.'

'And you work as a waitress in the evening?'

'Yes Aunty, all in black and a frilly white apron. It is great fun and good money.'

'It is above board I hope? You read such things these days.'

'Oh yes Aunt.'

I told her about my employers and my fashion studies and the girls in the house.

'Lunch is just about ready. If you girls would like to use the downstairs to wash your hands, I will pass things through the hatch to you. I will go and rouse your uncle. Since he retired he does nothing except read the Times end to end.'

We did as bidden. We took dishes from the hatch and set them on the table. Uncle arrived and kissed us both and said absently, 'Nice to have young women around,' I thought a bit pointedly as though he was getting at my Aunt.

I observed her, just 60, she had been ten years older than mum and had married George, a man 15 year older than her. She seemed exasperated by him and I wondered if he was suffering from mental degeneration. He knew enough to help us to white wine and him to a beer he kept in a crate on the unused tiled fire grate.

When it came to eating he ate quickly, chewing as fast as a cat with something stuck in its teeth. He was finished first and said, 'That was very good mother, any seconds?'

'You eat like an animal George it is not good for your digestion.' She gave him seconds and offered us more. We both declined.

'Ah leftovers for tea, I shall have to take a constitutional this afternoon.' He said.

We helped clear and pudding was produced, apple charlotte and custard. George ignored his dessertspoon and used a serving spoon to eat, as he always did. He had told me when I stayed, 'Best way to get seconds.'

We took coffee in the lounge having piled everything into the ancient dishwasher.

'Well George,' Aunt said loudly, 'What do you think of Alex, now Zandra?'

'Glad she has cleaned herself up. Looked like a boy when she was here. Her poor mother would have been in despair.'

Apparently I had always been a girl in his eyes. In my topsy-turvy world, I found that really comforting, even coming from someone as eccentric as Uncle George.

We stayed a little while more and then excused ourselves. Aunty said she would tell the family, such as existed.

As I drove away, Jay said, 'Well that turned out to be a bit of a flat balloon. They appeared to think of you as a girl already.'

'It was something of an anti-climax. Perhaps my disguise wasn't as good as I had thought, yet Gemma thought of me as a boy, didn't she, because she seemed upset at what you'd done.'

'You were quite close at school weren't you, and at that time you had not told anyone of the inner you. She might have felt a bit cheated, let down that you had come out to me rather than her.'

'But I hadn't come out to you, you had just dressed me.'

'But you looked so convincing and once dressed, every word and movement said girl, even your voice altered. It was a shock for poor Gemma.'

'I'm sorry I have sort of lost our close friendship but she has her boyfriend anyway. And I have you, actually we are closer ever than Gemma and I. Can I ask you something?'

'Of course, we are, in the language we spoke at school, besties, aren't we?

'I do hope so. I could not imagine life without you. I know, we will go different ways, me hopefully into fashion of some sort and you I feel will be a great star one day.'

'So what is the big question?'

'Jay you are beautiful, feminine, witty, clever, a talented actress, but you have no boyfriend. Why? You must have had some good offers.'

'I have had one or two, but unless I find a real spark, I cannot be bothered. I have had boys rubbing up against me, going for my breasts and a hand up my skirt, and it is fine, a bit of a thrill, but when I get home, I think, so what, do I connect at a deeper level, and so far I have not found the spark to ignite the fire. Anyway, I have you, my project, by new bestie, my sister. I have fun, I like being with you and helping. And as an actress, I do not want a romance, a quick wedding and divorce six months later because we are working on opposite sides of the World.'

The next days went quickly. Under her tuition and two hours in the school each day, I was able to stay on in a canter, giggling, full of adrenalin. It was thrilling and I began to really enjoy the riding apart from being with Jay.

We still slept together and I found her mother knew. I was quite embarrassed, but the family just accepted it. I learned a lot about being a girl, doing my nails, and my hair in different styles, trying out looks from Jay's extensive wardrobe. The contrast with my life three months ago, even six months when mum and dad were still alive was unbelievably different. I had been saved.

I had promised to resume my waitressing so got myself packed. To my surprise I found that Jay was coming too. She would be there for me during the day and when I returned at night. Her bedroom as the main leaseholder was the largest with a double bed and we decided we would keep sleeping together. These were truly happy days.

Chapter 20.

All was well in my life. I saw my GP each month for a new prescription of oestrogen and an injection to stop any vile further male developments in my body. I could not have been happier. My housemates were all supportive, even when they knew that Jay and I shared a bed. We assured them that it was not a sexual relationship but like two sisters. Whether they believed that or not worried me but not Jay. We know the truth she said.

Sue now had a boyfriend and I said again to Jay, surely there are boys you have met that you would like to be with, but she said no, she had met no one.

The end of year came. I had designed and made up three new outfits, this brought my year to six made up designs, a reasonable number for the June fashion show which was by invitation only and all sorts of fashion people came, from fashion houses, magazines and buyers.

I was awarded one prize for my wedding dress and a highly commended for an absurd and impracticable evening dress. That is the fashion industry valuing imagination and creativity over sense and wearability.

The summer holiday loomed and I had no idea what I was going to do with myself. I was invited to go to my aunt, an open invitation, but it was such an eccentric household that I was not keen to stay for more than a few days.

By the end of term I had discarded my breast inserts, my own breasts having developed enough for at least an A but bordering on B cup. With a B push up bra I looked reasonably full. The girls were impressed. They watched my development with interest, like older sisters.

End of term we had a party before going our separate ways, a few boys came and I danced with a couple if jigging about is called dancing. I had invited only Charlie from the fashionistas. I was surprised when Jay said she didn't like her. Anyway it was fun, my first real social evening as Zandra. Jay and I danced together most of the time. She was a very inventive dancer, doing character dances, from Arabian to Indian, from Latin American to a waltz, I never knew where we were going next, but it was such fun.

Jay was going to France to their villa near Bordeaux and invited me for a month. I was not sure I should impose on a family holiday but I then received a call from Dom reinforcing the invitation.

'OK, if you really mean it Dom, but no interrogations.'

'Oh that is all in the past. I know now, I heard what you said and I have done my research. You are just an attractive girl to me now and Sis really wants you to come. It will be nice for her to have female company and you two get on so well.'

'You are very persuasive Mr Lawyer Dominic. I'll come, a month in France, then I think I will come back here and live in the house, carry on waitressing and earn some money. Guiseppe and Gino will be pleased they are only losing me for four weeks.'

'I suppose you are coming back to be with Charlie?' Jay said.

'Whatever makes you think that?'

'I thought I saw a little spark between you?'

'No Jay, not for me, though she did say, 'if I ever wanted a walk on the dark side once.'

'See, I was right.'

Was she just teasing or what? Perhaps a walk on the dark side would be fun. I instantly forgot it.

The holiday was arranged. We would go in their two cars, so I would not have to drive. Jay was over the moon and hugged me tight.

'That is awesome,' she said, in her fake American accent, 'no really truly brill. I am so pleased. We can swim from the villa, just a few steps to the beach, and we have a small pool too.'

'A swimming costume might be a little revealing, I mean I still have something down there even if I am now OK on the bust.'

'What can we do, there must be some way?'

'There is a thing, something trannies use. I could get one and see.'

'Or a costume that has a little skirt, there are some in now.'

'I don't think that would do. Oh god how I hate that thing down there. The sooner I get rid of it the better.'

'How long have you to wait now?'

'Another eighteen months at best. They are pleased with me, I am studying and working as a woman, and they see that mentally I am stable. I have a good support network too and they say I look good. Everything in my favour except the length of the waiting list.'

'But they still say it will be eighteen months?'

'Yes, I know it is not long but I just can't wait to be complete. You may have noticed that I never let you see down there, that I never look at that part of me. I hate it; have done for as long as I remember. At school I used to go away and hide and............don't hate me if I tell you.'

'Of course I won't hate you.'

'I used to burn it with a cigarette or put a needle through the skin.'

'Self-harming, well that is common enough even in people with lesser problems than yours were.'

'You are not horrified?'

'No, of course not! You were in pain, undergoing mental torture. Zandie, I will never judge you for anything. You don't self harm now?'

'No, that all finished after the day I arrived and you sorted me out.'

'Thank goodness for that. Send for this thing and let's hope it solves your little problem.'

'The good thing is with the anti-androgens and oestrogen, it is a smaller problem than it was.'

'And if the surgery is not for say three years, what would you do?'

'I just have to wait. If I had money, I could go to Thailand I suppose which is supposed to be the cheapest and the sex change capital of the World. The best is probably San Francisco; the cheapest of all and safest is here in London the National Health. I know, patience.'

'Yes darling girl. You are doing super well, honestly, come admit it, everything has gone pretty well hasn't it? Just that one act of nastiness at college, otherwise people have been great.'

'Yes. I even had a letter from mum's cousin wishing me well. Yes, I have to say, most people have been great.'

'Then come it is just this bathing costume thing. Let's go shopping, you will need some beach wear anyway, a couple of sarongs and I suggest a costume and a couple of bikinis, then you can wear the tops and a sarong over the bottoms. A Beach towel and a sun hat, a wide straw, we can probably buy that out there, some beach shoes and flip flops, they are really good because the sand just falls out, perhaps a bag to put your sun tan lotion, makeup, book or e reader and anything else.'

We did the shops and got nearly everything, including new sun specs. I was going to buy some I saw for only a few pounds, but Jay said they did not suit so we roved from one multiple to another looking for '*the*' pair. When it came to things like clothing and specs, Jay was a severe critic. I was still learning how not to shop like a boy and buy the first cheapest. I was learning to be very self critical as I looked in the little sun spec mirrors holding the stupid label out of the way to really give the look consideration.

Eventually we found some she actually liked on me. "Yes, they are the ones!' We were in JL, our last chance shop, more expensive than the cheapos I would have bought, but I had to admit, as Jay said, they were so San Tropez. She just makes me giggle.

Jay also bought a few things and made me also buy two new black bra and brief sets, quite expensive, another blitz on the bank, but I was well pleased with my purchases and more than satisfied. I would do an extra night at the Kettle to pay for it.

At home I cut off tags and labels, laying everything out on the bed, revelling in seeing all my new girl things. Whereas a natal girl would have just been pleased, I saw these as further proof of my feminine status. This was reinforced by my darling Jay saying I would look gorgeous in them.

At the café Guiseppe and Gino had given me head waitress status as older hands had gone. I was allowed to open bottles of wine and present bills and even accept payment using the portable card machine if Gino was elsewhere. I still enjoyed it and it had become easier as the months went by.

At last, the day came to depart for Jay's home. I looked forward to seeing the boys again and her father, but I was still a little wary of Samantha. Her father controlled a business, but Samantha seemed the more formidable, no nonsense, and quick to judge. I don't think I had offended, but then she had never given any indication of approval or understanding of my situation. Of all the family, she was the only one I feared.

We adopted the same sleeping arrangements as last time. Four days later we were off to France in her parents two cars.

Chapter 21.

We arrived after dark at the villa in L'Amelie, up on the western, ocean side of the Medoc, settled in and ate a scratch meal, having had lunch en route. It was now accepted that Jay and I would share a bed, so we had the second double and the boys took the larger of the twin bedded rooms.

'Are you sure your mum doesn't mind us sleeping together, I mean, I know we are innocent but some might think the wrong things.'

'What, that I am having an affair with my cross-dressing boyfriend with the little tits or having an affair with the shortly to be lesbian as soon as she has her bits removed?'

I was unaccountably shocked by both descriptions of me, then I looked at her face and the impish smile playing about her lips and eyes, and I burst into giggles.

'Yes, when you put it like that, it does seem utterly ridiculous. I am so sexless at the moment, physically and mentally, I am no danger to anyone.'

'Oh my Zandie, you may think yourself sexless, I am sure no one else does, pretty lady.' We cuddled until we slept which was quite soon.

We awoke late and lay cuddled together. There seemed no rush to rise. We were all tired after the drive and Samantha had decreed that we would rise in time for a buffet salad lunch.

We two were up in time to walk to the shops and buy cold meats, tongue, ham and cooked cold salt lamb from Normandy. We picked up Roccammadour and Reblechon cheeses as well as some ripe Camembert, fresh salad, tomatoes cucumber and spring onions and lastly some game and paté pies and country bread.

Samantha ordered us about and we soon had the table sorted under the porch awning, overlooking the pool. The boys were already in the water, lean and reasonably muscular. Samantha commanded they put T's on before sitting to eat.

It was a relaxed meal, badinage between father and his sons, teasing of us girls by all of them, Samantha maintaining her status as referee when it got out of hand and was quite protective of me. In the cool of the evening we walked the beach for miles it seemed, small waves lapping the sand, the sun setting over the sea in brilliant red orange and gold. We played tag, catch with a ball Gerry supplied from a pocket of his ample shorts and linking arms taught the boys the 'Madness' walk. Gerry and I waltzed and so did Dom and Jay, then we swapped partners.

We ate soup and bread and drank some local wines and went to bed. That was the pattern of the days, relaxing to a rough timetable. Occasionally we would go to a larger town, twice to Bordeaux, sampling clarets, sauternes and graves in the wine cellars. I would swim early or late in the sea, once with Jay and the boys when the sun had disappeared over the horizon and we were covered in phosphorescence. When we tried to repeat this magical effect, there was no brilliance at all.

The days rolled into a week and then a fortnight and suddenly the days of idle pleasure were over and we were again packing the cars to return.

Home again I made my thanks and set off for the house, to get back to work. I would be on my own while Jay saw other friends and rode her horse. As I said goodbye, I cried. It would be the first time we had been parted for six months. I would be in the house alone, sleep alone and fend for myself. For some reason I was terribly afraid. Evenings working would be fine. I just wondered what I would do during the day.

It was not as bad as I first thought. I worked until eleven so by the time I got home it was half past, then I would watch some programme I had recorded, go to bed and get up around ten. I would breakfast and tidy up, do any washing I had and look after myself.

Sometimes I went into town and window shopped, other times I sketched down along the river or in the house drawing dresses, looking for designs I could use in the coming third year.

It was the fourth day of the second six-day shift I was working before Jay returned. I left work at eleven fifteen for the walk home on what had been the hottest day of the year. Even at that hour, there was still a glow in the sky, that beautiful deep pastel blue with azure shades where the sun had set. I could feel the heat emanating from walls that had been exposed to the sun in the afternoon. There were still people about, peacefully going home. The smell of a hot summer's day in the city lingered and from the roses I passed by and even stronger, wallflowers, traffic fumes, melting tar and creosote from the fences. I loved the smell of summer.

I turned down the alley that was a short cut to our street and noticed someone behind me. I walked more quickly but before I could break into a run, a hand gripped my shoulder and I was swung round, a fist crashed into my face and I fell with a scream and carried on screaming as I was kicked three times in the side. I took the first in the ribs but instinctively curled up taking the blows on my arm.

There was another shout and my attacker ran off. I looked up and found a couple with a dog bending over me.

'Are you OK love? Stay where you are, we are phoning for an ambulance. My wife will stay with you and I will go to the road to flag the paramedics.'

I tried to rise but the pain in my side was horrendous and I collapsed with a groan. The woman put something under my head, and I think I fainted again.

I don't know how long I lay there but eventually two paramedics were bending over me, feeling my pulse and inserting a cannula into my arm with a drip and they said morphine. I felt slightly nauseous, but out of it, conscious but woozy. I was rolled onto a stretcher and carried down the passageway to an ambulance.

The next I was conscious of, was the bright light of the hospital interior as I was wheeled along. I seemed to have to answer lots of questions. They asked if there was someone they could phone, next of kin, friend partner. I managed to give them my mobile with Jacquie's numbers. They cleaned me up and sent me for X rays. From there I went to the side room of a ward. I was given more morphine and fell asleep.

I awoke to find Jay by my bed, holding my hand.

'Hello you,' she said and kissed my forehead gently. 'Do you know who has done this?'

'No I didn't see, a man, quite large. It was quite dark down there and as I turned, he hit me in the face.'

'You haven't been robbed as far as I can see from looking in your handbag. He didn't even take your phone. The police want to speak to you when you are ready.'

'I'll speak to them now. But stay with me won't you.'

'Are you sure you can see them now?'

'Sooner the better, then I can go to sleep again.'

She went to the door and said something quietly that I could not hear with my face bandaged.

A man came in about thirty, dark short hair and a not unhandsome face, spoiled by a little moustache.

'Miss Zandra Gregson? That is your name?'

'Yes.'

'Can you tell me what happened?'

'I work at the Old Copper Kettle. I wasn't in a hurry to get home because I was on my own in the house we share.'

'How many live in the house?'

'Four, us two and Gemma and Sue.'

'And they are away at the moment?'

'Yes.'

'So you leave work, at what time?'

'Just on eleven fifteen.'

'So you said goodnight to your employers and left alone?'

'Yes, like usual. We waitresses go when our station is cleared. I am senior and usually stay to the end.'

'You get on well with your employers?'

'Guiseppe and Gino? Yes, brilliantly.'

'They know of your past.'

'Oh for months. They are both charming.'

'So your walk home is quite normal?'

'Yes, at this time of year there is still a glow in the sky, people about. I was just another girl going home.'

'Dressed in a black mini skirt and heels.'

'Yes, respectably, my skirt is not that short, in any case, he did not try to molest me in any way, no hand up my skirt or on a breast, he turned me, punched me in the face and I fell to the ground, then he kicked me in the ribs and my arm.'

'Did he say anything?'

'No, I don't think so. I heard shouting and some people with a dog came to help, then I passed out.'

'Do you have enemies? I mean you are, if I can be frank, in a vulnerable minority.'

'I am a fashion student. I came out nearly six months ago. They have been fine. It's a course that accommodates misfits like me.' I said defensively, picking up on what was I thought his prejudice.

'I didn't say that. It is a fact that gay and trans people, as well as young men and to some extent, girls are all vulnerable. Transgender people are more at risk because not everyone understands.'

'I'm sorry.'

'No need. So no enemies?'

'Yes she has.' Jacquie said. 'She had one of her creations unpicked just before the spring show. Luckily she had time to rework it and the rest of the students helped out. One student was sacked.'

'Oh that is interesting. What was their name.'

'John Ainsley.'

'Anyone else?'

'No, everyone has been fine.'

'OK, we will follow that up. You haven't come across Ainsley since?'

'No never. It may not be him, I mean I haven't seen him and didn't see my attacker.'

'But there is no one else bears a grudge.'

'No.'

'Thank you Miss. You have been very concise and helpful. I hope you are soon on the mend. I'll keep in touch.'

He departed and Jay sat by my bed and took my hand. 'Well done, got that over.'

'What has happened to my face?'

'Broken cheekbone. They say it will heal completely, you will have some swelling for a time, but your face will revert to what it was. You have two broken ribs.

They are painful but not dangerous. You have no internal injuries they say.'

'When can I go home?'

'They want to keep you in today just to monitor you in case there are complications. I will collect you tomorrow, but I want to do a few things today and I'll see you this evening. Before I go, is there anything I can get for you?'

'Some magazines to read and the TV, I think I need to pay for that and my bag, can you take anything valuable, just leave a few pounds and my makeup.'

'OK, I will be back in a minute after going to the shop.'

She returned with Vogue, Cosmo, Elle and OK.

'Thank you Jay. Thanks for everything.'

'Oh by the way, I have insured your car for me, so I can drive us about. Bye now and leave those handsome doctors alone.' She kissed me and I tried not to smile. It hurt. 'Or nurses!' She said. I wanted to laugh but it hurt more. She was gone and I slept.

Chapter 22.

Next day I was released into the care of Jay. She asked where I would like to go?

'What? Do you mean to sleep or to eat or what? I don't want to be out like this.'

'The choice is my parents home, until you have recovered or to the house?'

'Will your mum mind if we go there?'

'Don't be silly, she loves you in the same way she loves her own, just mum is not very demonstrative in that affectionate way dad is. Is that what you want to do?'

'I'll have to get some clothes and things first.'

'Of course. Let's go then and pack some things. You can relax at my parents' out of sight.'

'What about Guiseppe? I should tell them.'

'I already have. Said you would phone and let them know when you are fit. That is what we have to concentrate on now.'

We drove to the house and I sat in the car while she packed for me. My ribs hurt too much too contemplate climbing the stairs. She returned after what seemed an age, bearing a suitcase and makeup bag and a few odds and ends like my e reader and a book and pad and pencils.

'I think I have everything. We can always drive back if we need to. Are you ready to go? Can you stand an hour's drive?'

'I hope so, if you don't throw us round the roundabouts too fast.'

'Why would you think I would do that? You have never seen me drive.'

'No, I haven't, that is what is so worrying.'

'Then just lie back and hold on tight. I am kidding. I will be gentle.'

And she was, not slow, but sure, waiting for a good gap before entering a roundabout, so we did not have to accelerate like mad. We were soon on the rural roads of Suffolk, sunlit fields and quaint cottages. In just over the hour we entered her home drive and slowed to a halt by the front door.

I was surprised to find Gerry there, carrying my case in. I was lead to the drawing room and installed on one of the couches, made as comfortable as possible. Jay gave me more painkillers and a glass of water. She placed the TV remote on a side table, my books there too and asked if I would like tea or coffee and biscuits.

I asked for tea and fell asleep before it came.

When I awoke it was late afternoon and I found Samantha looking at me. 'How are you Zandie?' She had never used the affectionate of my name before.

'It's good of you to let me stay Samantha. I just hurt a lot, my side and my face, a bit of a headache.'

'I have informed our GP and he will visit this evening on his way home just to make sure you are OK. Is there anything I can get you? A drink? What would you like?'

'Water I think please a jug and a glass and I need the loo so can you help me up.'

She did so and as I struggled out of the settee, trying to stifle my groans, she said, 'I am so sorry this has happened. You know I do so admire you.'

'Why?'

'Well you have adapted to your new persona so well.'

'Not really Samantha, I have just revealed the true me. Before I was acting the part of a boy, not very well, not happily, a part forced by birth upon me. Now I am the girl my brain always said I was.'

'Yes, that is probably what I should have realised.' She accompanied me to the loo off the hall. 'Don't lock, just in case and I will stand guard.'

I used the toilet, managed to wash and dry my hands and found her waiting to help me return to the drawing room.

She lowered me back carefully. 'You do know that Jacqueline loves you, don't you?' she said.

'Oh she is such a good friend. I love her too.'

'No, you mistake my meaning, she really loves you, yearns for you to return that love. I know you love her as you would a sister. Do you love her as a lover too?'

I was in utter confusion. 'I don't know, I mean, we have never done anything like lovers do?'

'You mean you have never enjoyed sex together.'

'No. We sleep together but it is just like two young girls might do. We like waking up together and cuddling. I suppose it is all very immature, like eleven year old besties would do.'

'Dear Zandie, you are really quite innocent and immature aren't you. My darling daughter is what one calls a lipstick lesbian, did you not know?'

'No Samantha, truly I did not. Are you sure?'

'She makes no secret of it. Your housemates know, or at least so she tells me.'

'Do you mind that we sleep together? Is this what this is all about?'

'Oh I am too much of a realist to put objections in the way of her love. No I am resigned to her sexuality, I mean you know how much that cannot be denied. There is no pill to cure lesbianism. If that is how she has been born, then I love her just the same as my two boys. I just thought it time you were aware how she feels. If you cannot return that love in the same way, then there would be a difficult decision that would break her heart. She would recover of course, but it would be hard. Something to consider. I thought you ought to know.'

'Yes,' I said my face burning. 'I don't know. I am nowhere at the moment, not fit to love anyone, hormones whirring around my bloodstream. Am I attracted to men? I have not wanted to throw myself at your sons nor any of the boys at work, hetero or not. I love girls because I relate to them. I don't really understand men, how they even put up with being male. I love her, I know that and when we are apart, I think of her a lot. I owe her everything. I think I would not want to go on without her, but I know I would, somehow. If I lost her, I would be lost too for quite a while. Where is she now?'

'Riding, I was delegated to be nurse. Well I have made you aware. If you were holding back, because of what our family might think, there is no need. That is my message to you. I am going to bring you some homemade soup, French toast and some tea.'

'Before you go, I need to say something too. Thank you to you and Ralph, for your hospitality and including me in your lovely family. I have landed in paradise; you are all such good company, so considerate and inclusive. I do love Jay, I think I will return her love in the way she wishes, but until I am whole, I just don't want to have sex.'

'We are pleased to have you here. We love you, not just because you are Jacqueline's girl friend.'

When she disappeared I switched on the TV. Pointless was on, a panel game where one won by selecting the most obscure answer.

It was Jay who brought my tea, still in her riding gear. She kissed me on my head. She looked divine.

'Hi has mum looked after you?'

'Yes Jay, your mum has been very good to me. Did you have a nice ride?'

"I did, I am really back in the saddle. I rode with a girl friend from the village, Patricia. We used to go to Pony Club together.'

'Oh, that's nice.' I found myself feeling jealous.

'Now I wonder whether it would be better if you slept in your own bed tonight?'

'Don't you want me with you?'

'I just thought with your injuries, you might be more comfortable. You can do as you like.'

'I'd rather my servant slept with me,' I said with a laugh.

'Oh good! Your servant would rather be at hand too. I'll not bother to make up the bed in your room then.'

'No Jay, I want to be with you, so Patricia doesn't sneak in.'

'Would that matter?'

'You know it would Jay bird.'

'Jay bird?'

'I have always thought of you as a beautiful bird.'

'Oh, am I beaky?'

'You know you are not. I can't explain why I feel you are like a bird except that the first time we met, you reminded me of a beautiful gentle bird.'

'OK. Can I sit with you without hurting you?'

We sat together. I leaned into her, as that was the most comfortable for my ribs.

We sat watching the programme, trying to answer the questions. Some were really obscure.

I caught her watching me as I spooned soup into my painful jaw. I put out my tongue at her. She laughed. 'Beginning to feel better then.'

'Jay, I love you.' I said.

'You surely know I love you.'

'Yes, I think I do. I know you do. Just be patient with me will you? Don't run off with Patricia, you'd break my heart.'

'Oh! So you know how I feel?'

'Yes, I just wonder that I am worthy of you.'

'You muttonhead. If you weren't worthy, would a dish like me love you? Silly girl. I'm going to change. I'll unpack for you, and mum has bought you a present. I'll leave it on the bed.'

Chapter 23.

The doctor called about seven. He checked me over and wrote a prescription for painkillers. There was little else he could do. Time and my own body would now be the healers.

I struggled up to bed immediately after dinner, the boys doing their best to support me, but every step hurt.

On my bed was a beautifully wrapped package, a box tied with a broad pink ribbon with Fenwicks, Bond Street logo. I opened it to find an ivory silk nighty with shorts to go with it, by Chantal Thomass. Jay helped me undress and wash and I dressed in the new nightie. It was beautiful, lovely smooth seductive material and lace trimming.

Over the next days I slowly recovered, by no means fully but enough to move about. I had made the newspaper, no photo and happily my gender status was not mentioned. It said simply 'a twenty year old woman'.

My relationship with Jacquie had not altered, Yes we slept together but as I had told her mother, it was like teen or even preteen besties who just needed to feel the security of another in their bed. Her mother's words were very much in my mind. I loved her. The thing was how did I love her?

After two weeks my ribs hardly hurt unless I lay on that side. The swelling in my face had disappeared but there was a yellow stain left where the blue bruise had been. I knew that would disappear given time, I hoped my face would return to what it had been before the attack. All this time I felt Samantha was watching me, observing my relationship with Jay.

The police had failed to make an arrest. Ainsley had an alibi. The more I remembered about that evening, the more certain I was that Ainsley was my attacker. It came back to me in flashes, the hedge blurring as I broke into a run, the darkness of the pathway and the one street lamp twenty metres away where the footpath between hedges bent to the right, the silhouette of a face as my shoulder was gripped and I was wrenched around. It could have been Ainsley.

I walked alone or with the boys, when they were home or with Jay when she was not on her horse, recovering my confidence and healing my wounds. I could not ride; the movement would have been too much for my ribs.

The police interviewed me again, asking whether I had remembered anything more. I had not, other than the flashbacks, but they did not help identify my attacker.

Jay was just the same, loving, attentive. In bed she never tried anything except what we always did, a cuddle and a kiss, sometimes on the lips, mostly on my cheeks and forehead. I responded in the same way, I always had responded in like manner.

I remembered touching her, her hand guiding my finger into her most private place, explaining the intricacies of female anatomy better than any of the books I had read. I wondered whether that had been seduction or whether it was just caring, educating an aspirant female. I could not decide. Either way, it showed love. That she had not made any further move to seduce me, demonstrated her love and her respect, and especially her personal powers of restraint, if what her mother said was true.

Samantha on the other hand was much more friendly, calling me one of the family, including me in family chats and plans.

After three weeks I said that I thought I ought to return to the house. Samantha would not hear of it.

'Until the swelling has gone completely, you are not going anywhere young lady. We love having you here and if you go so will Jacqueline, and she is having so much fun riding. You wouldn't deny her that would you?'

'Oh no, I just don't want to outstay my welcome.'

'Good. I have tickets for the theatre next week, The English Ballet Company dancing Tweedle Dee and Tweedle Dum among other pieces. And I also have tickets to the opera, and that is a dress up occasion. By that time you should be beautiful again.'

'A dress up occasion, I haven't got anything as fancy as that.'

'What about one of your creations?'

'I have a choice there of a wedding dress, a cocktail dress or a quite ridiculous evening dress.'

'Have you photos?'

'Yes, well Jay has, on her phone if she has not deleted them. I have on my laptop but that is not here.'

'And they were made to fit you, you said. Could you get them in holiday time?'

'They are in the Fashion department. I can phone and see.'

'Well let us see what we have here. You must be the same size as Jacqueline and she has several dresses. Let's go up and take a look.'

She gripped my hand and I could not resist. In Jay's bedroom she opened the wall-to-wall wardrobe and I saw dresses there I had not seen before. Samantha pulled out four.

'Try them on.'

I hesitated.

'Oh you are shy. I will avert my eyes.'

'No it's OK, and I will need help.'

I stripped to bra and panties putting on a waist slip. 'Lets go.' I said.

She picked up the first, emerald green, floor length, and strapless. The material rustled seductively. I stepped in and she pulled it up. I held it by the bust cups and she zipped me in.

'Breathe out, make your chest as small as possible.'

I did so and she drew the zip to a stop.

'Can you breathe?'

'Yes, it is a bit tight but I could get used to it.'

'Look at yourself in the mirror.'

I moved to the full-length mirror, the dress rustled.

'Wow, I like it. What do you think Samantha?'

'It is comfortable?'

'It's divine. I love it, but will Jay want to wear it?'

'She no longer can, too big in the bust. The bust is a little big for you, but we can fix that. I think that will do and we are sure to have a stole for your shoulders. There, problem solved. I would still love to see your creations though. Turn round and I will unzip. Just remember, to pull your shoulders back and keep a straight back when you stand.'

I dropped the dress and stepped out. 'Thank you. I am so lucky to have met Jay and her family.'

'I'm sure she thinks the same, we all do. We'll leave the dress hanging out to air. Let's go down again as soon as you are ready.

At that moment, the door opened and Jay entered in stockinged feet.

'What are you two up to?'

'I just tried on your emerald dress for the opera next week, I hope you don't mind.'

'Oh that. Well I bulge out at the top, so why not. I would have liked to see it on. I'll have to wait till next week.'

She started to strip, throwing her riding gear into the linen basket.

'I'll leave you two together and start dinner. You can come down and help when you are ready.'

As she went, she closed the bedroom door.

'So bonding with mummy?' She looked at me sideways as she stepped out of her panties. 'Oh I'm taking a shower I stink of horse, but don't go, I haven't seen you all day. Were you like that, in your undies with mum?'

'Yes, to try on the dress.'

'Try it again, for me.'

She held it for me to step in and I wriggled it up. She started the back zip. 'Pretty sexy wiggle you have there.'

'You are laughing at me.'

She drew the zip to the top. 'No, I mean you have a pretty sexy wiggle.' She turned me, so we were face to face. Her eyes were mesmerising.

She held me by the waist. 'I can't keep this secret any longer. I love you, I mean really love you and want to be with you. I have been thinking about you all day. Now I suppose you will pack and go.'

'Were you talking to your mum about this?'

'This morning, in the stable.'

'And you thought you couldn't tell me.'

'I was afraid to.'

'Yet you know I love you.'

'I know you love me like a sister.'

'I can't love you like a sister, because I have the wrong parts still. I can barely touch what I have myself; I would hate it if you did. We sleep together and I have never touched you except that one time and you have never touched me, thank goodness.'

'I wouldn't would I, the lipstick lesbian of Little Lettingham.'

'Then kiss me, properly, on the lips.'

She did and I was so aroused I made her stop. She looked crestfallen.

'No it is my fault, I was so aroused that my auto responses started, and I feel so ashamed of that. I don't want you to see that. But if you can put up with me, I would love to be your girlfriend.' I was blushing.

'Darling you have made me so happy.' We kissed or I should say, she kissed me, her tongue penetrating my lips and meeting my tongue. I was aroused again. 'I'm going to shower. Shower with me?'

'You'd see me.'

'Wear your bikini bottom.'

'Can you let me get in the shower first and come in a minute later?' I asked.

'Of course.'

I entered the shower in my bikini bottoms, my breasts there for her to see. I played cold water on my penis and slipped a rubber band over it, hoping that cutting off the blood supply would stop erection. Bloody thing was such an embarrassment. She entered as I had turned the temperature back up and it was suddenly too hot. We both shrieked and dodged out of the water stream, bumping together, her breasts against mine, our stomachs together.

The water returned to a satisfactory temperature, and she moved us into the torrent and held me and kissed as I had never been kissed before. I felt faint, possessed and powerless and it was delightful.

'That was the best moment of my life.' I said.

'At last, I have wanted to do that ever since we started sleeping together.'

We dressed and descended hand in hand and entered the kitchen to help with dinner.

Samantha looked at us critically. 'So I heard a shriek, and by the look on your not so innocent faces, it has happened at last.'

'Mummy, you want to know too much.'

'What can I do?' I asked to change the subject.

'Can you make pastry?'

'I can.' It was fun being in this family. I was no longer a guest it seemed.

Chapter 24.

We went to the ballet and it was just brilliant, so clever and humorous. There are not many humorous ballets but Tweedle Dee Tweedle Dum danced to the Frederick Ashton choreography, was clever witty and colourful. I had first seen it on YouTube. I sat forward in my seat, drinking it in. It only lasted a few minutes but was for me the highlight of an evening of short pieces. The costumes were bright, primary and pastel and that added to the humour of the piece. Two more or less identical fat boys dancing together had to be funny.

Samantha rubbed my back and the other side of me Jay held my hand. I was so happy, never happier.

Another few days passed and it was the opera in Covent Garden. We dressed in our best frocks, me in the deep emerald and my highest four-inch heels that just kept my skirt from sweeping the floor. Samantha lent me her pearls and a pearl evening bag, something I had not yet afforded.

Even the boys cleaned up, appearing in black ties and dinner jackets, their father Ralph looking very handsome. Our transport was a surprise, a Mercedes stretch limo, with champagne and canapés. I wondered at the expense, but I found out that this was their silver wedding anniversary. It was typical of the family to generously include me in all they did. They had not told me it was a special occasion because they did not expect nor want me to buy a present. 'We have everything we need dear.' Samantha said.

We arrived at the theatre in true style therefore and paparazzi snapped us just in case we were important. Jay posed, using the opportunity to perhaps get her face recognised. She chatted to one of the paparazzi. She grabbed my arm and pulled me to her.

'This is my friend Zandra, she will be a famous fashion designer one day. Remember the name Zandra Gregson.' We were snapped together.

We entered the Theatre, holding our skirts to ascend the steps. The family knew one or two people and spoke to them as we progressed towards the Dress Circle, where we took our seats and awaited the overture. The orchestra tuned up and then as the lights dimmed they commenced the overture to Nabucco.

Much of it went over my head, as I have always thought about opera in general, some is not very tuneful, but the slaves chorus brought tears to my eyes. Jay put her arm around me and offered a tissue. I dabbed my eyes. The set was magnificent, huge blocks, looking like stone and the slaves perched all over them. It brought the house down. My first opera and although much of the music was not to my taste, the occasion and spectacle were just breath taking and one that I will never forget. On the way out I threw my arms round Jay and kissed her, 'Thank you.' I said.

Afterwards we spilled out on to the pavement and into the limo and were whisked away to The Ten Room at the Café Royal in Regent Street. I felt like a princess. We had the most delicious food and wine, a claret, Pomerol, that was just so fruity, and a Barsac, Chateau Climens with the sweet course.

They educated me about these wines as they were served and I resolved that in future I would not just take wine for granted and buy vin plonk, I will try to find out more from Gino so I know one grape from another.

I thanked my hosts for giving me such a treat and including me in what was a family celebration. For me it had been the best day, sitting next to my lover, watching and listening to a great work of art, enjoying witty conversation, such delightful company, entertainment and food. I was tired but never more contented.

The journey home was uneventful. We went straight to bed, unzipping each other from our evening dresses. We climbed into bed together and kissed goodnight. Life was beautiful.

We slept in late. Whereas before we had consciously not touched, now we wanted to explore each other. There was much to learn about loving a woman, and she taught me, where to touch and how to touch, how to kiss even. I was a complete ingénue, had no idea at all, how to please or be pleased.

My whole being had been so consumed with the unhappiness of being in the wrong body, that I had never experimented. While other kids from thirteen on were trying things, first kisses, having first sexual encounters, first love affairs, I had not. I could not have loved a girl as a boy and no boy would have accepted me as a girl, because I plainly was not one.

This liaison with darling Jacquie was my first love affair. It was essentially the first real love I'd had since about the age of five. Father had lost interest in me, mother was prevented as much as possible from as he called it, babying me, giving cuddles and kisses and had me sent away to learn to be tough aged eight. Boarding school had been devoid of any affection.

I had one good friend, Kenneth a lovely boy who called me Alexis in affectionate fun, I think seeing the girl in me but not being frightened by it, or ashamed of showing me friendship. The three years there seemed an age and a report I read after my parents death, kept in mum's bureau, described me as a somewhat effeminate child but reasonably popular. A note from the head master stapled to it had read, 'I believe Alexander needs special care and perhaps should see a psychiatrist.' It had not born any fruit, probably because father would not have admitted his son needed psychiatric support or assessment.

Mother somehow managed to prevent my going to senior boarding school, so I was sent to the local Comprehensive.

What I craved all those years in 'big school' was female company, not boys. In a way, being in a mixed school was more painful than being in a boys' only. All around me were those I wanted to emulate. I hankered after school dresses, pigtails, girl's games and chatter. Gemma lived in my road so we knew each other before. She had been my bestie until I was sent to boarding school and now we were together again in senior school.

Other kids thought us strange. I was certainly not a boy boy, but by keeping a low profile and ducking confrontation, I managed to escape the worst of the bullying which happened to anyone, the least different. Difference in my fellow pupils could be as little as wearing specs, being pretty, even saying thank you and please, or just smiling, something I often did. It was like Lord of the Flies, where the savages rise to the top and make life hell for the week or the intelligent.

Gemma wasn't strange or bullied, well perhaps a little due to her friendship with me, but ours was not the ultra affectionate relationship two girls might have. She was popular among her group and I was a sort of honorary member due to my association with Gem. That gave some protection, because our little band of swats and nice people stayed together, prepared to fight with our tongues and stick up for each other.

My dear Jacquie had given me the kind of affection, the love that two girls can share, platonic sisterlyness, unconditional, and she had shown me that an intimate relationship could be mine. And now we were lovers too.

My injuries had healed, the swelling in my face had all but gone, and the discolouration had faded enough to be covered by makeup. My ribs still hurt but no longer to any extent.

After her morning ride I told Jay that I thought I should go home and get back to work at the Old Kettle.

'I was thinking as I rode that you would say this. I want to come with you if you don't mind?'

'Of course I don't mind, I'm not going to meet Charlie! I hate to tear you away from riding and Patricia and enjoying the countryside, but frankly, I need the money and also, you will probably say nonsense, but I do not want to outstay my welcome. Your mum and dad have been so good to me, almost like the parents I should have had, but I do not want to be a sponger.'

'You are not, but I know what you mean. The thing was, you really had nowhere else to go, and you needed nursing. So we will pack tonight and go tomorrow after lunch. That way I can have a ride in the morning and you can work tomorrow night if they want you to.'

'Thank you Jay. I will ring them and see. One thing, would you be able to collect me after work, in my car.'

'Of course! I'll come sometime after ten and have a coffee or something while I wait. You mustn't ever walk home alone again.'

I went into Bury and bought flowers for Samantha and the largest most expensive box of chocolates I could find. As I was passing a tie shop I suddenly had a brainwave. I bought Ralph, I have never used his first name when speaking to him, an English Rugby Union tie because rugger was his passion among sports.

It was settled then. That evening I said my thanks. Samantha was lovely, I was no longer in doubt about her, and actually they had all been brilliant. I nearly broke down thanking them.

Next day after lunch we said goodbye. I hugged the boys and Samantha, and she kissed me in the same manner she treated Jay. That made me so happy, I really felt I belonged and mattered. We set off and were in the door after three-thirty.

We shared a bottle of wine at home. We made our bed and romped, my lessons in lesbian love continuing. We giggled and wrestled, teased and kissed. The good thing for me was, I discovered, when she played with my burgeoning and painful breasts and her kisses. She was very playful, it was fun, and I even stopped worrying about what was between my legs. Oh yes I still hated it, but Jay seemed able to ignore it completely. The other good thing was that it had stopped reacting something that would have sent men into depression.

The days developed a pattern. In the morning we would do things together, shopping, a walk by the river, maybe even a film or visit to a pub for lunch. In the afternoon we tended to relax.

At five I got ready, Jay insisted on doing my makeup and I readily gave in. She wanted to drive me to work, but I said that was not necessary, I could walk and while it was light I needed to get my confidence back after what I had been through at Ainsley's hands for I was now convinced it had been him.

I usually walked through the Mall across the Market Place and down the Parade and there were lots of people about.

The two Gs welcomed me in true Italian manner, three kisses from each and big hugs. They wanted to make sure I was well and then acquainted me with what was going on, two new items on the menu and three reset tables booked. Most nights in summer were hectic.

If I was lucky, customers arrived on time, and did not take too long to decide on the menu. I like children but when there were no children on my tables, life was easier. Youngsters were always more demanding, sometimes picky and slow eating and frankly made a mess.

My beloved would arrive at ten fifteen, take a spare table and I would serve her with a glass of house white and a prawn starter, given me by Gino for 'your driver', he said.

Bless him, these fearsome Italians, looking as though they had stepped out of a Mafia movie, were sweet and accepting of me.

My lover always drove me home. I washed the smell of restaurant away and climbed into bed. We cuddled, legs intertwined, her hand on my breast and mine between her thighs.

At the end of September Gemma and Sue returned. It was back to our studies.

Chapter 25.

The first good news on resuming my course was that Ainsley had been arrested. He was on a charge of GBH, grievous bodily harm, for punching a gay man in a pub. I rejoiced because my recollection of the night of my attack came in flashes and the person who crashed his fist into my face, was someone of Ainsley's shape and size. Could I have sworn it was he in a court of law? No. However, as I rethought the months after my coming out, working in the Fashion department, he had made several remarks that were unfriendly and unaccepting, using sarcasm as a weapon.

In my life, being small and obviously different, I was used to such verbal denigrations and had developed a deaf ear, that being the easier way out than confronting people and being beaten up. There is nothing a bully likes more than a challenge from a weed because it excuses, at least in their eyes, a violent reaction. I'd had enough dead arms, dead legs, punches to stomach and kidneys over the years, to wish to avoid more. With Ainsley, I had tried to maintain a feminine dignity, merely pretending I had not heard or was contemptuous of the remark. There is always one.

That he was arrested of course did not mean that he would be charged, detained or convicted. Even if convicted, when once he would automatically have suffered jail, now he was likely to be out on probation, tagged, doing community service or just let off with a warning. My fellow students had gathered from the grapevine, that I was the woman attacked in the summer and seemed to think I was now safe from Ainsley. I smiled and accepted their good wishes but I suspected that I was anything but safe.

Jacquie insisted that we go most places together, well we did anyway, but I went to college on my own and off to work too. She always collected me at night.

Nothing much had changed in the house. Sue was very on with her boy and we didn't see much of her. She was either studying in her room or out with him and his crowd. Gemma had finished with the guy she had been dating, James. Too full of himself, she said, and she had booted him off the field, her words. She had buckled down to her course, her final year to gain a BA in Law. She thought of going on to do Criminology.

'Does that mean you will be able to catch my attacker,' I asked playfully.

'Not until I get my Sherlock Holmes cloak and deerstalker.' Came the quick response.

The second good news was that neither Sue nor Gemma had turned a hair about my relationship with Jay. 'We discussed it,' they said, 'but only from the point of when it would happen.'

'It was inevitable wasn't it,' Gemma said. 'She made you her project right from the start. I am not criticising, she just saw in you what I had through familiarity missed. We had been friends from five years old. When we went to big school, we fell together. I just thought you were a gentle boy, mildly interested in girlie things. Jacqueline latched on to the hidden you immediately.'

'She helped me in with my things when I arrived here and saw something she shouldn't have Gem, my little supply of girlie undies. When she wanted to play with my hair and then makeup and dress me, it was like a dream come true, like I had prayed for from the age of four.'

'Oh and I never knew. Gosh you are deep, being able to hide your feelings like that. When you were in my bedroom in the hols, it must have been torture, seeing my girlie room and dresses, my dolls and makeup. I remember I once painted your nails and I was sure you liked it, but you said nothing. Why?'

'I was frightened if you saw the real me, that would be the end of the one real friendship I had.'

'It must have been torture, me having all that stuff that you coveted so much. Zandra, poor you.'

'Poor me. No, I am not asking for sympathy, in a way, my joy now makes all that longing worthwhile. While some girls find puberty worrying, I am revelling in every moment. My enjoyment of becoming a woman is probably more extreme than any natal female would experience. Anyway although my life will not be perfect, only being born in the right body with all parts working would make that so, I am now fine.'

'So you are happy, I mean really happy, as a pre-op woman?'

'Yes. Only one thing could make me happier, being born again as a girl.'

'Not being born as a contented boy?'

'Yuck, who would want to be a boy?' I said.

'You can't even imagine someone male being content as male can you?'

'No. I was so unhappy, I can't think how any man can be content.'

'I think I am getting it. It has taken a time for me to accept entirely, because I knew you so long as Alex. I'm glad we have talked; we haven't much, for a long time. And your relationship with your beloved actress?'

'Love, I love her, madly, passionately. I grin when I catch sight of her, like a Cheshire cat with cream.'

'Yes you do. Your whole face lights up when she walks in the room. If only I could find someone to love me half as much as you love her.'

'I have always loved her but it was her mother, Samantha, who told me she loved me more than platonically. I am devoted, besotted.'

Her eyes searched my face as if looking for any doubt. 'You do don't you, really love her, I mean lay down your life for her. Well I am pleased for both of you and I have to thank her for helping you so much.'

'You don't like her? I hope that isn't true.'

'Who could dislike our actress bird. No, I am just sus, that she will up sticks one day and leave you standing at an airport, and that will be that. I am afraid of the effect that will have on you.'

'Oh! We have spoken about that. Most English actresses make their way to the States eventually and it could mean that we part forever. I mean look Carey Mulligan, first saw her in Pride and Prejudice and then starring in an Education, the Great Gatsby. Now the toast of the USA. I would be upset, but I could not hope to stand in her way nor wish too. I know I am unworthy. I think actually, I shall never have a life long partner; I am not qualified. It is hard enough for a 'normal' person to have a lasting relationship, but for me? She would have to be truly exceptional. What I'm having done to my body makes me near female, not a complete female, at least in my eyes.'

'Now you just listen to me Zandie. You look adorable, your figure is more feminine each day, you act like a woman you are gentle and graceful. After surgery you will be able to have sex with a man if you so wish or a woman, your dear Jay. What will you not be able to do?'

'I will not have a period. You may think that a good thing, to me it is a sign that I have not quite made the grade. I shall not have children, I mean bear children, become pregnant, and those two things are the most basic acts of a woman. Oh yes I can look beautiful, wear lovely clothes, act like a woman, relate to them, but there will always be that small hurt, that something in the wiring of my brain, something in the very centre that went wrong, male hormones destroyed me as a female pre birth, and here I am, living a compromise.'

'Hey Zandie,' she cuddled me, 'I am so sorry. I just assumed everything was lovely. I thought that changing your body cosmetically, wearing lovely clothes was enough. Are you sure changing is right for you? Is this compromise as you call it, good enough?'

'It is a compromise but also as good as I can get. Oh yes, don't doubt that. I was self-harming all my teen years. I don't do that now. I love my makeup and dresses and at least being taken to be a woman and treated as one, is brilliant. You have no idea the difference it makes, the difference in being treated as a woman rather than a boy. Don't doubt that this is right for me please. I think sooner or later I would have killed myself had I remained male; it was like a sentence of death. And one thing I tell myself, that there are natal women out there who also cannot conceive for one reason or another. So much can go wrong with reproduction, I am just another victim.'

'Gosh, I never understood at all did I? All those school years, I never guessed the pain you were in. Were you envious then of me?'

'Oh god yes, of every girl, even the fat ugly ones, because I thought I could do so much more with their body than they did. Some girls should not be allowed out, like one I heard the other day, on Woman's Hour, an arch feminist, Doctor Sinn something, trying to say that young children should not have hormone blockers and their transgender feelings were the result of gender stereotyping. That old chestnut wheeled out when the medical and psychiatric world gave up on nurture years ago. She, an arch feminist women's libber, looked like a bloody man, yet didn't want boys to become girls.'

'Hey you feel so strongly about this don't you?'

'I had a role model. My father was a man's man. He was not unkind to me, he just expected to have a normal boy and he got me. I don't think mum treated me abnormally at all, I am sure she did not. Yet from age three, before I even knew what a girl was or looked like, I instinctively hated my body and wanted girl's clothes, and toys.'

'Wow. I never understood. If I go on to do my Master's, I may make this my thesis. It is so interesting.'

'Thesis on what?'

'On the Law affecting transsexuals and transgender; on the incidence of assaults and deaths. On suicides. I shall never say this again Zandie, but if, for any reason, you feel desperate, you will phone me, talk to me.'

'What makes you think I will contemplate that?'

'If a lover lets you down, if you feel life has not given you enough joy, whatever. People do get desperate you know.'

'Like when I was at the end of my tether with Aunty and her eccentric household you mean or if my beloved Jay rockets away to super-stardom. I don't think I have made the wrong decision and Jay, well, I know this won't be for life. I would like to think she finds utter fulfilment and I don't think I am it. I think I am being realistic. As long as I have a few friends, like you, I shall be OK. I never want to lose touch with any of you, but certainly dear Jacquie and you, my lovely Gemma. Can we hug?'

We hugged.

Chapter 26.

Summer had faded seamlessly into autumn and suddenly it was winter, an icy wind blowing out of the Fenland. We woke to shivering cold and dialled the thermostat up. Indian summer had spoilt us, now winter was seeking revenge for its delay. The ground was white, pavements trickily negotiated in women's shoes. It was too easy to skate on a heel. Therese in Fashion appeared with a leg in plaster.

Jay and I cuddled up, whether on the sofa or in bed. Our love had not waned, even though she had been away for two weeks in late October, at Pinewood doing Persuasion, the part of Louisa. This was a big break for her and I was thrilled too for myself, the trans girl friend of a TV star, but realistically, I prepared myself for her loss. It has been good, I told myself, but nothing that good can last forever.

It would only be a matter of time before she would appear in a British film proper and then be picked up by the States, Broadway or Hollywood. I steeled myself and made the best of our present time together.

She had not changed towards me. She was generous, treating me to drinks and meals, the odd little present of jewellery, clothing or makeup. I was in essence a kept woman. I protested from time to time, but she would not be denied, she had money and liked treating me. I wondered whether this was to salve her future conscience. She would be able to tell herself, she had treated me well after she had flown away and left me. It was a dishonourable thought of mine.

I worked away at fashion and I'd had an approach from a lesser Paris House, to go to work there after College, whether or not I obtained a degree they said, they liked what they saw, and a piece of paper, a degree was of no account. They wanted flair and imagination.

I looked up the House, Levrais; they had been quite big in the seventies and had fallen, as others had come up. Such is the fickle nature of the fashion industry. Now they were looking for young flair and imagination and where better to look for that than in England?

I told Jay about it.

'Then we go over as soon as we have Christmas break, have three days in Paris then go to mine for Christmas.'

'Your's for Christmas? Are you sure? Have you checked with Samantha?'

'Mummy has assumed that we will be together. She didn't think she needed to issue an invitation. Of course, we are lovers, it is expected that we will be together. So we break on the seventeenth. On the eighteenth, that's Wednesday, we drive to Ebbsfleet, leave the car there, get the train. Daddies PA will do it all for us. All you need to do is arrange to talk to Levrais. You do have your passport?'

'Oh yes, I have that of course.'

'Good it is settled then.'

That was it, Christmas break all arranged. What I would have done without Jacquie, I just don't know. Gemma may have invited me for Christmas or not, but now I did not have to worry.

'Oh and by the way, we are skiing over new year.'

'Oh you will enjoy that.'

'No silly, *we* will be skiing, all of us including you. We own a chalet, well a half share, in Val d'Isere. You said you skied.'

'Oh I do, not for two years but I do, quite well, one thing dad was pleased about.'

'And you have kit? Ski suit, etc.'

'I have, had, I guess I need to buy new, girl gear, right down to boots.'

'Of course you do, how dim of me, I was just thinking you have always been you, as you are now. Then we must get jacket and trousers. You could hire boots and helmet.'

'I could.'

'What is the matter now.'

'Just, am I really welcome, I mean your family, I am an interloper.'

'Hush girl. Zandie, we all love you, the boys included. I tell you what; we will look on the Internet tonight, and see what kit we can find cheap. We get the train, it is brilliant.'

'Jay, you are so lovely, I just feel sometimes like I am your wife, you make all the arrangements then tell me.'

'Oh. I had not thought, not considered, I just thought I was doing this, like Christmas and skiing, and just assumed we would be together. You are my girl friend!'

She looked at me with her so intense gaze, as though looking into my soul. Taking my hands in hers, she said, 'I'm sorry, of course I should ask, discuss. I just assume that we are together and do the same things. I should not take you for granted.'

'I know you are always thinking of me and I love you for it, and I am acting, well, just like a wife I suppose, asking to be included in the making of plans. It is all fine, I am being silly, but I sometimes wonder that your family really want me as much as you say.'

'They want you because I want you. The boys have each other, but they could bring girls. I have you, you make my life richer. I can't imagine not being with you. You know mummy likes you, I mean it was mummy told you about my sexuality and said I loved you.'

'OK, dear Jay, thank you, and your family, of course I will come and it will be lovely. I just find your generosity so unbelievable. Perhaps I undervalue myself. You know I love you though, you do not have to spoil me.'

'I love *spoiling* you, seeing you blossom into a lovely girl.'

'Hug darling Jay.' We kissed.

'Don't undervalue yourself. You look wonderful, you are intelligent and you are a nice person. Just because you have a handicap, it does not mean you are unlovable. I just think of you as a girl, my girl friend, you are no less than you would be to me, if you had been born with say, a withered arm. Loosen up and be confident. Now these arrangements, Paris to see Levrais is it? Christmas with mum and dad and then skiing. Is that all right?'

'It's much more than that, it's super, brill, wonderful and so are you.'

'Good.'

Chapter 27.

Three weeks later and I found myself on the Eurostar, premium class, with a fancy meal as we raced through the green countryside of Kent. In no time we were through the tunnel and into France. My sweetheart sat opposite, composed and beautiful. I hoped I looked half as good.

We ate the meal and consumed the tiny bottle of wine and glided into Paris Nord past the dreadful North Parisian architecture of multi story flats and cheap industrial buildings. Baron Haussmann would turn in his grave.

A taxi took us to a hotel on Avenue Franklin Delano Roosevelt. The entrance was between two shops, but once inside it was spacious and ornate, with lots of gold mouldings and marble. We checked in and were taken to our room by a bellboy.

This was luxury indeed. The bed was enormous, a king, apparently her father's favourite room, he always took when in Paris. The bathroom was equipped with thick and fluffy towels, robes, perfumes and bath salts.

Jay unpacked and I followed suit. 'Right,' she said, 'here we are. My girlfriend and I in Paris, city of love.' She threw herself into my arms and we kissed passionately.

'Tomorrow we see Levrais, so let's go out now, see something, and have dinner and an early night.'

We walked to Champs Élysée, then to the Arc de Triomphe. The queue was short so we joined it and in ten minutes were climbing for the best view in Paris. We could see all the way to Notre Dame, up to Montmartre and the Sacré Coeur, over to La Défense and to Tour Eifel. It was stupendous. We went hand in hand from one side to the other, marvelling at a city so beautifully laid out.

We browsed the shops on Rue du Faubourg and found a nice little French restaurant and then it was home to bed. I looked through my portfolio, just checking that everything was in order. It looked OK to me. Next day at ten I would see them and find out what they have in mind.

Next day after breakfast, we caught the Metro to Convention nearest to Levrais workshop, to look round and meet designers and cutters, then someone would take me to their Rue Faubourg shop and out to lunch.

I was extremely nervous, for one thing my French was only GCSE and I think my accent was atrocious.

We found the works and used the intercom to get access, that in itself proved a problem because they could not understand me. It did not help that Jay stood beside me giggling.

Eventually we gained access and wandered down a passageway to an office. A young woman met us and escorted us up stairs.

There we were met my André Moreau, head of design and I recognised him from the summer show. I had not expected to see him again.

He showed us the works, an enormous cutting room, with laser cutters and computerised design. There were racks of wonderful materials bought in for their next autumns designs, deep reds, oranges and lemon, teamed with black and grey.

Luckily André spoke good English, so we had no difficulty. We took coffee in his office and looked at the design suite. There were empty boards, they had let people go, he said, and were looking to leave haute couture to a certain extent and make inroads into the readymade mass market, selling designs rather than clothes to the High Street. Their customers would go to the East for manufacture he suspected. He shrugged 'the modern way.' He said.

He led us to the ground floor and we found a taxi waiting and we were taken over the river to their display shop on Rue Faubourg. It was large. In the office we were introduced to Simon Levrais who had recently taken over the business on the death of his father. My portfolio was examined again and they chatted in French and English.

Simon explained their interest. I would be as he termed it, a paid intern, all found, meals, travel, and accommodation, but only a small salary for a year and if they liked what I did, then they would give a substantial salary increase.

We walked to a restaurant for lunch. I was not completely sold, but it was interesting and I told them so, asking for time to think it over. There was no commitment on either side. They said that they would attend the end of year show six months away and see what I had produced. That was an incentive at least.

After a good lunch, we were free to go and we headed for the Metro and took a train to La Madeleine and walked to the Tuileries and crossed the river to Quay d'Orsay. We spent all afternoon among the Impressionists.

We took tea at Hotel George V and afterwards wandered the riverbank as far as Notre Dame, hand in hand, or cuddled together as lovers do. I could hardly believe this was my life, when a year ago, I was suicidal, still a boy, suffering the sudden loss of my parents. I was immensely happy and said so to darling Jacqueline.

'I'm glad. I am too. There is something I have to tell you though and I don't want you to be upset.'

'Oh. That sounds really serious.'

'I am in the running for a film role in the States, about a young English girl, newly arrived in New York, looking for love and fortune.'

'In the running?'

'Well, I have the lead if it comes off. They are still looking for finance.'

'That's brilliant Jay. So you will be away. When?'

'They talk about starting to film in October, so it would be up till Christmas.'

'OK.'

'I had hoped to be with you after we both graduate and I will be for a time, like if you get this job in Paris, I could be with you while you settle in. Will you be OK on your own for the autumn?'

'Oh sure. Look we both knew that this is an undergrad romance and I realised that with an acting career, you would zoom off to become a star.'

'I will come back to you Zandie, I promise.'

'No, don't promise, I want you to be free, but until then, can we just carry on as we are?'

'Of course, that is what I want. I love you Zand; really, this is not a passing whim. This is much more than a project. You'll see.'

'I love you Jay, but we have different careers, I may be here in Paris, you will be making your fortune in New York. Underneath my self-delusion I am a realist. I have known something like this would come and you are too brilliant not to succeed. Perhaps one day, you will be Dame Jacqueline Coles.' I smiled.

'Of course I shall be, and you too, Dame Zandra Gregson or will it be Dame Zandra Coles if we marry, couturier to Her Majesty. The newspapers will have tired of gossiping about us, they will simply say, Zandra Coles, couturier, accompanied by her partner, Dame Jacqueline attended the premiere of ......'

'That sounds nice,' I said, 'then we will toddle home and have hot chocolate with a tot of brandy and climb into bed in our flannelette nighties.'

'Never flannelette, I promise. But I do mean what I say.'

'I know you do, but you are going to meet loads of new people. I just want a promise that we will always be best friends.'

'That is easy, of course. And it will be much more than that. Come, home and bed. We have one more day and then home and Christmas, then skiing. It is all going to be super.'

Chapter 28.

The best Christmas yet, I could safely swear to that. For the first time ever, I received presents that I actually wanted, from undies outwards and most expensive of all, a pair of Christian Louboutin's prized shoes, but most precious of all, a friendship ring from Jay, diamonds and sapphires, set in a five millimetre gold band. Aunty sent me two hundred pounds, an enormous sum for her, saying I was to spend it wisely in my new life. I decided that I would buy ski boots and a helmet, rather than put my feet and head in ones that had been on numerous feet and heads.

Christmas with the Coles was a traditional affair, from hauling in the tree on Christmas Eve and decorating it, to opening presents on Christmas afternoon while drinking champagne. Ralph played Father Christmas, handing out the presents to each in turn and I found they had made lots of small parcels for me so that I never missed a turn. I received everything a girl could want, from perfume to panties. When I opened the small box and found Jay's ring, I nearly broke down. She took it and placed it on my finger and in front of the family kissed me on the lips. I blushed. I resolved that I would buy her a ring too.

Samantha went to tend the turkey and we said we would follow in a minute. Alone in the hall on our way to the kitchen Jay said, 'I know you don't believe me, but I will be yours forever Zandie darling girl. You have to believe me.'

I smiled and kissed her. 'I do hope so, but forever is such a long time. Let's not make too many promises my dearest sweetest Jay. I will always love you.'

She sang it back to me, the Whitney Houston song, hugged me and kissed me.

We entered the kitchen and Samantha set us to work, pealing and cutting, placing pots upon the range, making brandy butter, stuffing and making stock for the gravy. When everything was ready, there was little to do for the next hour. We washed our hands.

I was surprised when Samantha caught us both by the hand and brought us all together. 'Group hug,' she said. 'I'm so glad you have found each other, really. I love seeing the affection between you.'

We returned to the drawing room. The curtains were closed and we played games, a backgammon tournament, charades and rummy. We girls had to keep skipping out to the kitchen, but I did not mind. It was what I identified with, not lounging with the boys.

The dinner was a feast, crab and cucumber mouse, followed by turkey and all the trimmings, ending with Christmas pudding, mince pies, brandy butter, cream and ice cream. When we had cleared up, the boys washed the pots while the machine did the rest. We watched a DVD of 'White Christmas', the 1954 film a family favourite and then the boys put on some skiing DVDs of people doing extremely dangerous things.

Boxing day was leftover day, cold meats and salad, a long walk in the morning around their land, calling on the farmer who rented it from them. Whereas Christmas day had been dull and drizzly Boxing Day was bright with a rising wind. We returned home, refreshed, feeling that we had in part walked off the festive food and we youngsters played the game I hate most, Monopoly. To the boys' disappointment, Jay won. I was so pleased for her.

I kept looking at my ring, moving my hand so the diamonds sparkled and Gerry noticed and smiled. 'Well that present went down well,' he said and Jay looked and gave me a hug.

'Good, I am pleased. It means a lot to me too.'

Next day we youngsters went to a ski shop in Essex and I bought boots and a helmet, really pretty boots and a powder blue helmet to compliment my ski jacket. I was fully equipped. We went home and packed.

Next morning we loaded the cars for an afternoon departure to Ebbsfleet. We would catch the evening train and arrive at six in Bourg St Maurice. A taxi would meet us and transfer us to Val d'Isere. Life with the Coles was so full of love and excitement.

Jay and I had seats next to each other and we managed to recline them and sleep cuddled up. It was bliss, next to my love, hurtling smoothly through the night. We arrived in Bourg St Maurice still in the darkness of early morning, our taxi driver waiting, and we were soon winding our way up to the resort.

We were relieved to find snow on the road as that meant fresh snow to ski on. An hour later we were in the chalet, eating breakfast of fresh bread, eggs and bacon, coffee and juice.

By ten-thirty we were on the slopes, swooping down our first run of the day, the boys going frighteningly fast. It was very cold and we made several stops for vin chaud. The boys were always eating too.

At three-thirty we made for home. We were tired and the light had gone. The last run was down the Face, steep but quite boring, a test of fitness and endurance more than anything. We could see the town laid out below us, looking terribly small, a six hundred-metre descent with an Olympic time of just two minutes. We took several minutes more than that.

We ate out most nights, long skirts or trouser and boots, fluffy jumpers and silk blouses. Expensive but not amazing food, tasty dishes, rather than the epitome of modern cuisine. I usually went for local dishes raclette, tartiflette, fondue and myrtille tart. It was none the worse for that. After skiing, we needed feeding and feeding well. Tartiflette was my favourite.

I suggested to Jay that I could cook one night, as a thank you.

'You don't need to. In any case, can you, I mean it won't be spag bol or curry will it?'

'Oh damn, don't they like spag bol?'

'Idiot. OK so you are serious. So what are you proposing?'

'I thought watercress and celeriac soup, followed by steaks, veg and sauté potatoes, and choc fondant with vanilla ice cream.'

'Wow, it seems a lot to do. Are you sure?'

'I can make the soup the night before, so that is not a problem. I have looked and we have the tools. The veg is just put in the steamer and I cook the potatoes and steaks at the same time. The puddings I can make the day before and freeze and cook from frozen. They will cook while we eat our main course. It would be a little repayment for being here and I would really like to.'

'Would you like some help, I mean I am not a great cook, but I can prep the veg and possibly sauté the potatoes?'

'It would be lovely to do it together. I'll shop the day before.'

'OK, I'll tell mum we are doing it, and then she won't protest. If she thinks it is just you, she will say no because you are a guest.'

'I thought I was one of the family.'

'Ah, yes you are, my lover.' She slipped into West Country brogue, always the actress.

I managed to find everything I needed in just one supermarket except for the watercress. I finally found the missing ingredient in the smaller one, a bit wilted but for soup that did not matter. I made the soup before we went out to dinner and made the choc fondants when we returned, Samantha tried not interfere and Jay hovered.

'Oh! You do actually know what you are doing.'

'Oh yes, I have always cooked, one thing dad hated about me.'

On the night I served the soup and it went down well with fresh pain de compagne. The steaks were left till last and took just five minutes in a hot pan, served with a red wine sauce. As we ate, I put the fondants in. I served them and they came out perfectly, the centre molten and spilling out when cut, somewhat of a triumph. I served them with a raspberry coulis, cream and ice cream

'The best meal of the week,' said Dom. 'Well done girls.'

'It wasn't me, I was just sous chef, maitre de cuisine was our dear Zandra, her menu recipes and everything.'

'Well it was damned good,' Ralph said.

'Thank you Ralph,' I said.

'I have to congratulate you Zandra, really, a revelation. When Jacqueline is a great star, you will be able to entertain for her. I am jesting, but it was very professional and tasty.'

'A small offering for all your hospitality. I don't take it for granted. I am really grateful for your acceptance of me and your generosity.'

'We love having you and it makes my daughter so happy to have you here. Oh, you are blushing again. The boys will clear up. You come and sit by me. Oh yes, Jay as you call her can have your other hand. I have never seen such love birds.'

'Mummy, you are being really embarrassing.'

'Yes dear, but I am happy for you both.'

Two more days and we were back on the train. It had been a great holiday and I loved my new family.

Before we knew it, it was Easter break.

Jay and I returned early after Easter.

The house was in chaos. It looked as though we had been robbed and my wardrobe had been turned over. My waitress uniform, shirt and skirt had been cut to pieces.

We called the police to report a burglary but as far as we could see, nothing had been taken. My laptop was where it had been left, under Jay's bed, so the burglar had not searched thoroughly.

We waited in the car for it seemed ages before anyone turned up. At first the detective thought it unimportant, but when he found I had been victim of an assault his manner changed. He was he said, asking scenes of crime to attend. He gave us the name of a locksmith and advised changing the locks which he said, were inadequate.

We waited in the car another hour and two people turned up in a van. They dressed in white suits and carried equipment in. We sat and waited. After an hour the detective came and told us they had finished except to take our fingerprints for elimination. The lock guy turned up and changed the locks in about half an hour assuring us that these locks were superior.

By now it was dark. We locked up and walked to the Kettle. I explained what had happened to the two G's. They gave us a meal and I promised to work next evening.

I couldn't help feeling down and oppressed. I felt sure this was personal. There was only one person who was openly hostile. Ainsley.

'This is my fault.'

'Why do you say this?'

'Because it was my room that was trashed, my waitress gear slashed to pieces, and three dresses. I shall have to throw all my undies out. I feel violated.'

'But even if it is someone getting at you, it is not your fault. Now don't be silly. Tomorrow we buy you new stuff, new underwear especially, in case you know, they did things. And we go through your whole wardrobe and sort it out. If you have to have new, then that is what we do.'

'It will take all my savings, all the money I had put aside.'

'I know, but I helped before and I will help again. This time I will speak to daddy. It will be OK. And we should get insurance too.'

We went home and locked ourselves in. We drew the curtains and went from room to room, checking windows. We even looked in wardrobes and under beds. We made our double bed and showered together, me in my bikini bottom. We got into bed and cuddled, listening for any disturbance. Eventually and I do not know who was first, we fell asleep. When we awoke it was daylight. The day was sunny, the sky blue with tiny cumulus clouds. It was the sort of day when one thinks nothing can go wrong, an innocent day, Jay said. We hoped it would be so.

We breakfasted and then sorted through my stuff. We threw out all the undies except what had been in my case. Most of the other clothes were not my favourites and we decided to give as much as possible to the charity shop down the road, but made a list for the insurance and Jay took photos of everything.

In the afternoon we hit the shops, this time with her father's permission. Mostly I allowed Jay to pick things for me, trusting her judgement, after all she had more experience of dressing as a woman than I, and she had inherited her mother's good taste.

We returned laden with bags to find Detective Steve Wilkins on the doorstep.

'Replacing your stuff? Well, we got a result. Ainsley picked up his DNA on a glass in the kitchen. He had helped himself to a beer it seems, and then threw the can in the trash, silly boy. He's in custody now and we have charged him with your assault too.'

'Thank God. Will he be kept on remand or whatever you call it?'

'Right, remand. We consider he is dangerous. He thinks you are immoral, that's his excuse. He belongs to an ultra right Christian group; we found loads of books, tracts, and newspaper articles in his flat. Thought I'd let you know so you can rest easy.'

'Thank you Steve. We were a bit nervous. He'll stay in jail will he?'

'We hope so. Never can tell these days, the prisons are full, so they let all sorts of criminals out. But we can make a good case.'

After ripping off labels and prices, we put my new clothes away.

We made some supper and I dressed for work. I walked there on a lovely evening. I told Gino and Guiseppe that the police had made an arrest. The bookings were mostly early, so I was finished by half nine and phoned Jay. She picked me up, even though Ainsley was in prison. Christian right or not, we said, he had to be a bloody nutter.

Sue returned and then Gemma. Summer term and finals for all of us. Our life in the house was coming to an end. Gemma was advertising for new housemates as Sue, Jay and I would no longer be there in September. A number of possibles walked through the door and we all gave our verdicts after the interviews.

I had made my treks to the clinic in London every three months. I found that my name was gradually working up the list and they thought it would be October for surgery. That was difficult if I was to go to Paris, for Levrais had now made a definite offer. I had told them of my gender status, so there was no difficulty there. If nothing better came along, then I would take the position and do a year at least in Paris. It would look good on my CV anyway.

Jay said it would suit her to be based in Paris although if her career took off she could spend time away. It was inevitable that we would be apart.

I was surprised when Samantha called me. She said that Jay had told her it was likely I would be in hospital when she was in the states doing this film, 'The Girl Who'.

'I will take you to hospital and pick you up and bring you back to stay with us. No, no arguments, in any case, where else is there for you to go? You can hardly live in Paris while convalescent. I want you to be here so Jacqueline is not worrying about you.'

'Thank you. It is really kind of you. I accept of course, I just can't thank you enough.'

So it was all settled.

The end of year show saw me with three dresses in and this time I asked Jay to model all three for me. The first was a tea dress full skirted but dropped waist, very girly. The second was an ensemble, skirt, shirt and duster jacket and lastly an evening dress in wine red silk, slim fitting, ruched and pressed tight diagonally on the bodice. It went well and Levrais who were there again, confirmed their offer. I told them of my appointment with the surgeon, but they seemed not phased at all. They had expected it and told me kindly, to make sure I was fit before going to join them in Paris.

Suddenly it was the end of the year. Jay and I went to each other's college balls and danced shamelessly together. The Arts ball was a zany affair, with people in fancy dress of all sorts. After the euphoria of that, it was packing all our belongings so new people could move in. The four of us went for a last meal together, not to the Kettle; we wanted somewhere where we could misbehave a bit. We chose a smart restaurant and drank champagne, courtesy of moneybags, all evening. We were loud, giggling and tipsy and we intended to be.

'Do you have a date for surgery yet Zandie?' Gemma asked. And suddenly the party had become serious.

'They think end of September, but it depends on a lot of factors.'

'And you haven't cold feet?' Sue said, her glass of champagne half way to her lips. "I mean it is such a big step to take.'

'It isn't a big step for me. It's like for you, having a growth removed, a blemish that prevents you from being pretty.'

'Even though we have known you for nearly a year and a half, I still can't imagine what being you is like.'

'I know it is difficult, I mean you are happy as a heterosexual girl, as happy with your body as most people. Jay maybe gay, but equally happy with her body. It is as if I was born into the wrong body, with a female mind. Suppose you woke up and had grown a willy overnight. Wouldn't you feel revulsion?'

'Oh God, put like that. But you were born with it. Anyway, I don't think you were ever a boy proper, too girly, too pretty, too graceful.' Gemma said.

'Well if I woke up with a willy, I would give it a pull first, just to see what boys feel. I would give it a good try out. Then I would want it chopped off.' Sue said.

We all giggled ridiculously.

Jay calmed everything down by being serious.

'She is all girl to me already,' Jay said. 'I hope it will be September for your op, because in October I am off to New York for this film and much as I would like to be there.

Mummy is going to look after you, but I want this understood Zandra!'

'What?'

'No flirting with mummy, she is half in love with you as it is.'

I burst out laughing. 'Oh Jay, I shall never ever love anyone else but you. You are so clever, yet so zany.'

'Good, I'm glad you love me. I love you. I'll be there if I can. How long will you need for convalescence?'

'They tell me three weeks minimum.'

'We will all visit won't we girls?'

'Oh sure.'

'Of course.'

'You don't have to.'

'Don't be silly, of course we do.'

'No I shall be in London. You will be here Gem and Sue, well, I thought you were going to Cambodia or something. I don't expect visits, honestly. Just send flowers and a card if you want.'

'Anyway, we have the whole summer together don't we Zand, I will teach you to ride and we go to France and I know mummy has a few surprises for us too.'

'You two, like a marriage already.'

'Well, when we do marry, you are both invited.'

'We are not going to marry,' I said. 'Don't fantasise about that. The truth is I may be working in Paris, Dame Jacqueline Coles could be anywhere in the World. Too many show biz marriages come unstuck and she is going to meet so many glamorous people.'

'You read too much Hello and OK Zandra. These glamorous people have all been airbrushed and not only their photos. They are just people, who happen to have been actors or singers. Most have more frailties of character than the ordinary person because they have been spoiled, pandered to and flattered. Don't ever doubt my love again! Yes I am furious with you Zand, your bloody inferiority complex, I love you, you bloody dumb blond, dress designer.'

Her voice had risen and other diners were looking. Some sniggered.

'I'm sorry Jay, I am really sorry.'

Jay rose from her chair, turned and put her tongue out at the table behind that had sniggered and came to me.

'Bloody stand up,' she commanded.

I stood. 'Now kiss you dumb bird.' We locked lips and embraced. A few diners clapped, others shook their heads at two women kissing.'

A couple of men at an adjacent table watched. 'Well that was worth coming for,' one said.

Jay turned. She mock curtseyed. Before sitting down. 'Another bottle or home?'

'I think home Jay.'

'Then I'll get the bill. You can all pay me at home. Come along darling.' She held out her hand to me and we went to the till together, hand in hand.

Chapter 29.

The goodbyes were emotional and I have to say I cried. I was ending the best ever eighteen months of my life and I should think, anyone's life. It had been one long adventure, coming out, being openly trans, having treatment and studying something I loved. I have been a waitress, buying and wearing girl gear, and treated as a girl, with three beautiful girl flat mates. The best of all this, has been my beautiful lover and her family. Oh I took a beating and my stuff was trashed, but I would do it all again. It was like I had been reborn.

I ought to be apprehensive after all, in about three months I am going to lose part of my anatomy, but I am not. I am rather, like euphoric, looking forward to being whole by losing part of me. The thing that I have hated all my life will be gone. I wonder, in an idle moment, when I have nothing else to think about, what they do with the part they do not reuse. I suppose they will just sling it in a bin and it goes to an incinerator. Even that does not make me flinch, in fact I laugh, aloud.

My darling Jay looks up to see why I am laughing, and I hesitate to explain. 'Just thinking about the operation and I got the giggles.'

'I know what you were giggling about.'

'What?'

'I might be wrong, but I think you were wondering what they do with your bits?'

'How did you know?'

'I know you and I had wondered myself.'

'Oh, so I am not awful then.'

'Perfectly reasonable question. You could ask them to pickle it for you, keep it in a bottle of formaldehyde. Perhaps turn it into a bedside lamp. Or perhaps you could be a donor to someone going the other way.'

'Now I am no longer laughing. I don't care what they do as long as it's gone.'

'That's my girl.'

'Now the bad news is that they have brought filming forward so that they can make use of the Fall, the trees in New England, will be full of colour mid October. I fly out on 26th September.'

'OK, well we knew it was touch and go whether you would be around.'

'I'm so sorry. I really wanted to be with you Zandie.'

'I know you would be if you could, but this is your big break. I hope the film is worthy of you.'

'Mm, well my first proper film. I have the script and it is quite lightweight, a bit like some of those Jen Aniston movies, but I am the co-star. I can't afford to be choosey yet but I shall be when I have choices. Mummy will look after you. I'll get back if I can.'

'Jay I don't want you to, you have to concentrate on making this film. I shall be fine.'

'Well we have the summer holidays. I have thought if we went to France in your car, then we could have five weeks there. You could practice your French, because by the end of October, you will be in Paris.'

'Yes, well there is nothing to keep me here, but do you want to leave so early and forego riding?'

'Oh I shall have plenty of time for that, between films or when I am being a waitress because no one casts me. Look, it is inevitable that we shall spend time apart, we have to accept that, unless of course, I make it big and become a star, then you can give up work and just look after me.'

'Now that is an attractive proposition. I could design frocks for us to wear to the OSCAS. I know we shall be apart Jay. I shall miss you dreadfully. I shall just say this; I love you enough to want your success more than to have you close and unhappy. Now, let's think about France. I will have to get my car serviced and check on things like insurance. So we will be there on our own?'

'For a week at least, even ten days.'

'That will be bliss for me, like a honeymoon.'

'That's it! Why don't we get married before we go?'

'Because we can't. If I am married while still legally male, I cannot get a Gender Recognition Certificate without having a divorce. Then when I get the GRC, I would be able to marry you. I know it is crazy, but that is the law, and I can't get a GRC until I have had surgery of some sort.'

'Oh talk about a tangled web. So have I got this right? If we marry and you then have reassignment surgery, we would have to divorce before you could obtain this GRC? So then after getting the GRC, we could then marry? It's crazy. Why have a GRC?'

'Because without it I am still legally male under the law, with it I would be legally female and can change my birth certificate.'

'Bloody hell Zandie, they don't make life easy do they? This is hoop jumping.'

'Well I guess there is logic to it, and we cannot have just anyone adopting the role of opposite sex without some sort of commitment, otherwise every trannie would be up for duel sexuality, playing the laws off against each other.'

'So we will just have to keep living in sin. I quite like sin anyway, in fact I like it a lot.'

'Yes, but you know dear Jay, you have a reputation to protect. I wonder whether you should be too 'out'. People say it doesn't matter, but what do they say in private? I mean we became a bit of a spectacle at the restaurant. For me it doesn't matter, but you may become, hopefully, really famous. They may dig this up and throw it against you. Me, well my industry is full of offbeat people.'

She looked at me as though I had blasphemed before a bishop. 'I think you are wrong. I will ask my family what they think. I hope you are wrong. The joy I feel loving you cannot be bad, I mean I would sacrifice my life for you and I think you would for me. That cannot be bad can it? That sort of devotion to another human should not suffer censure or hate.'

'Perhaps I am wrong. Perhaps the intelligentsia are accepting. It is just the rest who hate difference. We live in privileged communities.'

'But your fans may not.'

'Yes but I will tell you why you are wrong, there are a number of gay stars and they are accepted.'

'True, gay people, not many transsexuals though.'

'No, because they are not out. If they were more out, perhaps they would be accepted. Anyway, Are we ready?' I nodded. 'Then we are off.'

We kissed Sue and Gemma goodbye, swearing we would meet up, but would we? I hoped so.

We had a week in Suffolk and then we were on our way to France. The whole journey was a revelation, the first time we two had been alone together, uninterrupted by others, for so many hours. From leaving Little Lettingham to arrival at L'Amelie was a full day. We caught the twenty-fifteen ferry in Portsmouth, had dinner and slept in our two-berth cabin. The boat arrived in France just after eight next morning. It was a beautiful time, and if it had been our honeymoon, it could not have been better.

We drove south, we two in my car, our little cocoon, in intimate privacy, two lovers, two on the outside of society but worthy members of that society and the human race.

Whether we would ever have a honeymoon was another matter. I decided not to think about it because I felt so negative. I just could not see that our relationship would survive our different careers.

At last after an uneventful drive we arrived in L'Amelie. We soon opened up the house and unpacked and had time to walk to the shops and buy basic supplies and fresh produce, fruit and veg, meat, cheese, bread and milk. We agreed to eat at the café in the village centre where the lorry drivers and tradespeople ate in the day and local French ate at night. Jay was known and gabbled away in French and I tried to keep up. She saw me straining to listen and slowed her speech, occasionally translating a few words into English. I got about half of it, but my brain was gradually acclimatising to the French language, so that it did not just sound like a stream of vowels and consonants, but became words.

Over the next days she refused to speak English at all and I began to pick things up. My accent was terrible and she would correct it, making me speak more nasally but also emphasising vowel sounds and rolling my R's. After the first week, she told me that I had improved and I knew I had.

We met a French girl, a language student hoping to go to Oxford and she told us that English has around forty thousand words but we mostly have ten thousand in day to day use, while the French have a smaller total vocabulary but use around fifteen thousand. I had always thought French long-winded, this probably explains why.

I cannot tell you without being really sloppy, how good that week was. We lived in bikinis except when we went into the village. I also wore a sarong for obvious reasons, but I told myself it would not be long before I could show myself in bikini bottoms. Next year I would dispense with the sarong.

Our days were our own, to walk the shore and call at a beach side café for lunch or morning coffee, to have the occasional swim or sometimes take the car and visit one or other of the hundreds of vineyards, because this was the home of Medoc and other clarets, of Sauternes and Graves and even some local sparkling wines.

We went to Bordeaux and spent the evening in the cinema, watching a French dubbed version of Pride and Prejudice, the Keira Knightley production, one of my favourites. Another night we lay in the park listening to a concert cuddled up.

Time passed quickly. I had thought ten days would prove a long time but it went by in a flash. The rest of the family arrived and the holiday changed, no longer a honeymoon when we isolated ourselves from other people, but we became again part of a family. The boys were brilliant teasing and provoking, sometimes quite serious too and surprisingly caring towards me. I recognised Ralph and Samantha Coles had raised three lovely children.

It was the last night of the holiday. We had all gone to dinner at the best restaurant, Cuve de Vin, and we were all quite merry. Jay was almost out of hand, teasing her brothers and continually kissing me.

When we went to bed, she insisted in undressing me. I allowed her to do my top half and she caressed my breasts and kissed them. She undid the zip on my skirt and allowed that to fall to the floor. She put her fingers inside the elastic of my knickers.

'No!' I said firmly.

'I just want to see what you will have taken away. I won't touch.'

'I don't want you to see.'

'Just this once. Never again.'

'You promise, no touching?

'Have I ever let you down?'

'No. OK if you must.'

She lowered my panties.

To my amazement, there was no erection. My penis remained flaccid, testicles were now small and the penis itself was more as it had been when I was twelve.

'It's small,' she observed. 'I would love to be in the operating theatre and see what they do.'

'Well I will be,' I said, trying to joke.

'Silly! I wonder whether they would allow me. Would you object? I mean it is no different than a husband being at the birth of a child, they are both very intimate occasions.'

I had pulled my nickers up and put on a nightie.

'Would you really want to? Anyway you will probably be in New York or New Hampshire or somewhere.'

'But if not?'

'Why?'

'Because it is a big moment for *us* isn't it. Not just you, us. I want to share this with you.'

I looked into her eyes and found only serious interest, beseeching and loving.

'OK, I mean they may not allow you, but we can ask if that is really what you want.'

'I do.'

The five weeks were over. It had been a glorious time, full of love and fun and I had got to grips with speaking French, slowly, ungrammatically and incompletely but at least I was speaking and understanding much more.

The summer rushed away. The Coles liked the theatre in all its forms and we went nearly every week, locally or in London, usually catching the train from Ipswich. We also did a couple of proms, getting me into serious music, a pop classic, Rachmaninov 2, played by Anna Federova and some more obscure pieces and a symphony, Tchaikovsky, The Little Russian. Both were glorious evenings. This was how their children had been brought up, to have a broad appreciation of the Arts.

Jay and I also went to all the galleries, Tate, both of them, the National and National Portrait Gallery and the Courtauld and the RA summer exhibition.

At the V&A we saw wonderful costumes and dresses. Jay was such a brilliant companion. She would have made an excellent wife for anybody, mannered, talented, cultured with a broad spectrum of appreciation and knowledge of the arts, she could hold her own in any society, yet she was, and I did feel this, wasting her talents on me. I dared not say so for I knew it would make her angry.

Chapter 30.

September and Jay and I went to Paris again, flat hunting. I had been given a rental ceiling figure by Levrais but Jay's father said he would subsidise a rental for a nicer flat if that would make Jay happy. In truth I think she had maneuvered him into it but I did not know how. At least it was a sign that she intended to continue our relationship.

We scoured the agents and walked miles. I wanted somewhere with a view, preferably of the river or a landmark, the Eifel, Sacré Coeur, Place de la Concorde. Yet we did not want too much traffic noise and in Paris, that made finding our bijou apartment difficult. We finally found one in Rue Jean Nicot, overlooking the Seine on the left bank opposite the Bateaux Mouches. It was only one bedroom, but a good size lounge, small kitchen and adequate bathroom. We both agreed it was super. I could leave my car in the street or in the Levrais factory garage.

The flat would be five minutes walk from Munsee d'Orsay. It was ideal.

The furnishings were sparse, but we could find things at the flea markets or second hand. The next four days were used to scour the shops and markets. We succeeded in finding importantly, a king size double and splashed out on a new mattress for it. We also found a

303

couch, old and a bit threadbare, but still comfortable and in a flea market a table and three chairs. The rest we could do at our leisure, or my leisure for I would be on my own for a month at least.

I hoped I could manage in a foreign city with no friends. I wondered suddenly whether I could cope with that.

I received the date of my operation, entry to hospital on first Tuesday in October. Jay would by that time have been away a week. Although the surgeon had given permission for her to attend, he showed disapproval. It now seemed she would not be in the country anyway. I was relieved and yet a small part of me wanted Jay to share in this whole experience.

'Oh well, I might have fainted. I will phone and Skype, so take your iPad. I want to be assured that you are OK. Course if you had a local anaesthetic you could Skype the action to me with the IPad.' She laughed.

I laughed too. 'You really are terrible.'

'I know. But seriously, I do worry, I will worry about you. That is why I so wanted to be there, in the room making sure they did everything properly.'

'I will be fine. You have to concentrate on acting darling. Honestly I will OK and your mother will look after me and keep you informed.'

I tried to work out a timetable in my head. I would be in hospital five days, then go to Little Lettingham for at least two weeks. After a follow up at the hospital I would go to Paris. It would be the last week in October at best. Winter would be just round the corner.

'When do you think the filming will finish?'

'They say they have a month, so the end of October for the location shots, then Pinewood. It should all be wrapped by end of November.'

'Oh!'

'Oh? And then you mean? Then I come to you and we come home for Christmas, mummy insists and I want to be at home then anyway.'

'Of course.' I was not looking forward to being so long alone. Work would be fine, but what to do in the evenings and weekends.

'Are you OK Zandie?'

'I was thinking, ' will use my spare time to decorate the flat.'

'You're scared aren't you, of being alone all that time. It is far from ideal. You have to promise that if things are not right, you don't feel well or happy, you tell me. Get on the train and go home to Little Lettingham.'

I nodded.

'No, swear and you tell me everything. Don't be a closed book like you can be. I will not accept when I phone and ask how things are, you just say fine. I shall worry if you do.'

'I promise. How could I deny you anything?'

'And we will be skyping, so I shall see your face.'

'And I yours my darling Jay. I love you so.'

'And I love you.'

September drifted away. I felt a rising tension. Jay went to Heathrow, her mother driving us. We went as far as passport control. We two were in tears, Samantha somehow maintaining control. We kissed her goodbye.

Four days later I entered hospital. Samantha took me in for seven am and I was prepped immediately and by ten I was being wheeled into the lift. I felt the canula go in, counted to three and woke up back in the side ward. A nurse was bothering me with silly questions, what colour was my hairbrush, how did I say my name? I answered. I had a drip she said and a bottle for urine. I must drink. If I had pain I must ring. I must ring if the urine bottle was full or if the drip was running out. I fell asleep.

When I awoke, I found my darling Jay by my side.

'How are you here?' I asked, still woozy.

'I flew over and I fly out tonight I have just six hours here from touchdown to take off, just brought clean knickers in my handbag. I had to make sure you are OK.'

'Darling Jay, I must look a mess. What about the film?'

'Torrential rain, they stopped filming, providentially. How do you feel?'

'Fine, no pain. I think they have done it. At last I am free I am liberated from that thing.'

'Is that how you feel?'

'Yes, it is as though a great weight has been lifted. I am whole at last.'

'I can't wait to see.'

I felt myself. 'I am bound up, trussed like baby, so you will have to wait.'

'I wish I had got here in time to see what they did.'

'Really? I don't think I could even watch a video.'

'I could, because I am emotionally attached to you and want to know what happens to you. But you feel OK?'

'I feel fine, a bit tired and sort of woozy still. I couldn't read at the moment, but it's early days.'

'Of course. I'll wash your face with wipes and moisturise you. Then if you can sit up I'll brush your hair. Would you like me to plait it?'

'Um, that would be good.'

She freshened me up and it made me feel much better. She plaited my hair one long plait. She took a ribbon from her bag; stars and stripes brought specially and tied it off.

Samantha appeared. 'It is time to go Jacqueline. I will take good care of her and you can skype. Now I think she should rest and you have a plane to catch.'

We kissed. 'I love you,' she said. They departed. I blinked a tear and I lapsed into sleep again. When I awoke it was dark. I switched on my bed light. I could here movements in the corridor and in the main ward. I rang the bell and said my bottle was full and the drip was nearly empty. I was reminded to drink. My temperature and pulse were taken. I slept again.

Chapter 31.

We had skyped each day, sometimes twice a day. Her film was going well and she was enjoying it too. I was strong enough after five days to be discharged; my wound healed enough for the dressing to be removed.

I went to the hairdresser in the hospital and had my hair washed, trimmed and blow-dried. I made my face and dressed and was ready for discharge. It was Ralph who picked me up at three in the afternoon. He was very solicitous and charming. I was so lucky. They are a family in a million.

We were soon home in Little Lettingham, Samantha wrapping me in her arms and making sure I was fit. Would I like a bed made up downstairs? Could I eat what she had prepared for them? Was I bleeding? How did I feel?

I reassured her on all counts. We ate dinner at six-thirty and I went to bed. Over the next weeks I followed the directions for my recovery, using the dilators, a task I hated, keeping myself clean with salt baths, taking longer and longer walks in the country side when the weather was clement.

Samantha was caring but discreet, leaving me to go to her. She was also very often at one committee or another, so I was alone n the house. I read and sketched designs. I skyped with Jay nearly every day, leaving it to her to contact me as she had a hectic timetable, dawn till dusk and thereafter, the stars met up and socialised.

'I have fallen in love with your mum.' I said.

'I knew you would. You are so fickle.'

My third week after the op, I went back to hospital for a check-up. They declared all was well. The post op tiredness had at last gone and I phoned Levrais to tell them I would arrive second of November.

That last week went quickly. Dom was home, Gerry was climbing in Scotland, so Dom saw it as his duty to entertain me. We did films, went to the seaside and walked, went to London once to see Phantom, his suggestion because I said I had not seen it, and walked some more.

My phone had gone dead it seemed, as Jay did not ring the three days prior to my departure for France.

On the day of my departure, she sent a text that just said, 'see you soon xx ☺'.

I drove to Dover and caught the ferry. The drive to Paris was uneventful and I managed to find a parking space outside my flat. I opened the main door with the combination and brought all my goods into the lobby. I locked the car and closed the lobby door. I jammed the lift and filled it with my stuff and squeezed in. I arrived at my fourth floor, jammed the door again and spilled everything on to the hallway. I took my key and opened the door. The lights were on. There was the smell of cooking too and I wondered if I had opened the wrong door. I checked the number on the door. Correct.

Jacquie appeared. 'Surprise!'

I cried, with joy. We hugged like for ages, feeling each other's bodies, kissing.

'Wow,' I said. 'Oh Jay, wow. That was the best surprise ever.'

I looked at her. She had changed, she looked more sophisticated, her hair was in soft waves, dark with subtle chestnut highlights. She wore a dark lipstick.

She looked at me. 'You look fine, perhaps a little tired, I suppose after your drive, but there is something different. That slight nervousness, like a trapped fox, that has gone and you look serene, cool. You are aren't you?'

'I am, at last I am complete. I just need a cervix and a womb transplant now, well and a few other bits.' We laughed together and hugged again.

'Can I see?'

'Of course,' I said, shamelessly. Well there was nothing to be ashamed of any more. I pulled up my skirt and dropped my knickers.

'Wow,' she said, 'good job. I wouldn't have known. Do you have any pain?'

'No, it's fine.'

'No hang-ups at all?'

'Would I have let you examine me there before?'

'No, too right you wouldn't.'

We packed my stuff away. Jay would be with me for four days, then off to UK for filming at Pinewood. It would take about three weeks. Then she would be with me until we departed for Lettingham for Christmas.

Tomorrow would be my first working day. All was well in my wonderful life. I checked myself in the mirror. I could see no trace of Alexander.

'Brill,' I said, pirouetted and fell into Jacquie's arms. Where better to be?

The End.

If you liked it please leave a review, it means a lot to hear your views.

Also written by me.

'Trudi', 'Trudi in Paris', 'Trudi and Simon', 'Trudi without Simon'

'A Strange Life', my autobiography of being a transsexual.

'A Time to be Brave', Thriller set in Essex.

'The Cellar', Police Procedural Thriller.

'Tina G', Teen thriller.

Made in the USA
Charleston, SC
19 May 2015